W9-AAZ-531

FALLING ANGELS

BY THE SAME AUTHOR

THROUGH THE GREEN VALLEY

FALLING ANGELS

BARBARA GOWDY

BLOOMSBURY

A portion of 'Disneyland' appeared in slightly different form in *The North American Review*, Fall 1988 and in *The Best American Short Stories* 1989, edited by Margaret Atwood (Houghton Mifflin 1989).

The author wishes to thank the Ontario Arts Council for financial assistance.

First published in Great Britain 1991

Bloomsbury Publishing Ltd, 2 Soho Square, London W1V 5DE

A CIP catalogue record for this book is available from the British Library

ISBN 0 7475 0708 2

10 9 8 7 6 5 4 3 2 1

Printed in Great Britain by Butler and Tanner Ltd, London and Frome

In a small-town suburb three teenage sisters, Norma, Lou and Sandy, are attending their mother's funeral together with their roaringly drunk father and a posse of local newspaper reporters. Sandy, the youngest and the beauty of the family, is leaning over her mother's casket. 'What are you doing?' Lou asks. 'Changing her lipstick,' Sandy sobs. Mother never wore pink lipstick.

It is the beginning of the swinging sixties and the sisters are negotiating their unsteady rites of passage. They study, date and try to keep their mother from jumping off the roof. When she's not drinking or flirting with oblivion, she watches television. Day or night she wears only nightgowns and never goes out, except on Christmas Day. The girls idolize and protect her but she is more like a beautiful ghost than a parent. Father, only tolerable when his extra-marital sexual dalliances absorb him, terrorizes the family with his mania for military discipline. Obsessed with the possibility of nuclear war, he builds a bomb shelter in the basement with money saved for a trip to Disneyland and forces the family to live in it for two agonizing weeks.

In FALLING ANGELS, Barbara Gowdy has created a world that is both unforgettably bizarre and disturbingly familiar. The three sisters, fuelled by terror and love, harbour the dark secret of a missing fourth child as they grapple with their traumatic and hilarious family skeletons. It is a novel that will resound long in the minds of all who read it.

To my parents for not being the parents in this book.

RESURRECTION

1969

All three girls are in the front seat, the fat girl with the glasses is driving. In the back seat their father is asleep sitting up.

They pull into the parking lot, and two men who are leaning against a blue Volkswagen van turn to look at them. One of the men has a camera round his neck. "Fuck," the thin girl says.

Their father jerks awake. Before the car has come to a full stop, he has his door open. "Scram!" he yells at the men. He falls out the door, onto one knee. The three girls quickly get out of the car. Their father stands up and heads for the men, thrashing his arms. "Vamoose!" he yells. "Bugger off!" The men don't move.

"Dad," the fat girl pleads. Their father staggers away from everyone and slaps his pockets for cigarettes.

"Just leave him," the thin girl mutters. She starts walking, giving their father a wide berth. Her sisters follow. The fat girl with the glasses can't squeeze between the fenders of the two hearses, and she reddens, conscious of the men approaching. "Climb over," the thin girl orders. Glancing at the photographer, she reaches into her purse and gets out the pack of cigarettes that their father is searching for. If she has to have her picture taken, she wants to be smoking.

The photographer starts clicking. But not at the thin girl. He aims at the third girl, the pretty blonde one, who is waiting while the fat sister climbs over the fenders. "Figures," the thin girl thinks. The pretty girl gazes at the scorched white sky as if wondering whether their mother is up there yet.

"Excuse me," the second man says, sauntering up. The pretty girl smiles politely. The thin girl narrows her eyes. The eyes of the man are rabid with fake pity. He says it's a real drag about their mother and he hates like hell to hassle them, but the pictures aren't going to have captions unless he gets their names straight.

Both the fat girl and the pretty one look at the thin girl. "Lou," the thin girl says. The man flips open a pad and starts writing. Lou nods at the fat girl, "Norma," nods at the pretty girl, "Sandy." This is the first reporter that Lou's let anywhere near her. It's because he has long hair and a beard and is wearing blue jeans.

"Still in high school?" the reporter asks conversationally.

"For another few weeks, yeah." Lou blows a smoke ring. The photographer goes on clicking at Sandy.

"When did you get the cat?" the reporter asks.

"What?"

"The cat. Your mother went up on the roof to rescue a cat, didn't she?"

"We better get inside," Norma murmurs.

Sweat starts dripping down the reporter's forehead. "I understand that one of you was there when it happened," he says, earnest now.

"We were all there," Lou says. Her hand shakes bringing her cigarette up to her mouth. "Okay, we've got to go," she says, moving around the reporter, feeling herself on a dangerous verge.

Inside the funeral parlor, Sandy asks where the washroom is. She has decided to put her false eyelashes back on.

It's not vanity, like Lou thinks. This morning Lou said, "You've got too much makeup on. Nobody'll believe you're broken up." So Sandy took her eyelashes off, but now she wishes she hadn't, and not only because of the photographer. She can't understand why someone as smart as Lou hasn't figured out that the better you look, the better people treat you.

She bats her lashes to see if they're stuck on. "Beauty is only skin deep," she tells herself defensively. She has always taken this expression to mean that only what is skin deep is beautiful.

Her throat tightens. She has had an awful thought. In an autopsy they remove all your organs, don't they? She isn't sure. But just the idea of strange men rummaging around inside their mother. . . . She thinks of their mother's organs sloshing in whiskey. She thinks of their mother's womb, and she starts crying and fishes in her purse for Kleenex. Even before their mother died, the depressing image of her womb crossed Sandy's mind a couple of times. She pictured an empty draw-string purse.

Norma and Lou go into the room where their mother is. Nobody else has arrived yet. They're an hour early because yesterday their aunt phoned and told them to be. The casket is against the far wall, between big green plants that you can tell from the door are plastic.

Norma walks over. "Is she all here?" she whispers. Only the upper part of the casket is open, and the lower part doesn't seem long enough.

"Who gives a shit," Lou says in a steady voice. "She's dead." Last night Lou cried her heart out. Their sweet little mother who tap-danced . . . have they cut off her legs? No way is Lou going to look in the casket.

She walks to the window and parts the heavy velvet drapes. Their father is yelling at the newspapermen again. They are about ten yards away from him, standing their ground. Lou can't hear their father, but the newspapermen are nodding as if whatever he's yelling makes a lot of sense.

Norma touches the tip of their mother's small nose. "It's me," she whispers. Their mother's nose is like a pebble, cool. Her face is white and smooth as a sink, and Norma realizes it's because the blood has been drained from her. "What do they do with the blood?" she asks Lou.

"Christ," Lou says, lighting another Export A. "Do you *mind?*" She wonders if Sandy went to the washroom to cry. In a couple of weeks Sandy plans to marry a guy who has the stupidest face Lou has ever seen on a person not mongoloid retarded. Lou suddenly has a panicky feeling that she has to put a stop to the wedding. As soon as possible. Today.

She closes her eyes. What the hell is going on? she asks herself. What does she care who Sandy marries? Maybe their mother is seeping out, and Lou has swallowed Maternal Instinct. People in Wales believe that you can swallow a dead person's sin. But their mother had no sin, and nobody can tell Lou that she sure had *one,* the biggest one, because Lou has always viewed that as a sacrifice. Their mother had no instincts left either, now that Lou thinks about it. Drowning pain Lou doesn't count.

When Lou opens her eyes, Sandy is entering the room on the arm of an undertaker. He gestures toward the casket, disengages himself and backs away, and pressing her hands at her mouth, Sandy walks over and stands beside Norma.

"She's got lipstick on," Sandy says.

"They always do that," Norma says.

"But she never wore pink lipstick," Sandy says, her voice breaking. She slowly brings her hand down and touches her fingers to their mother's lips. "Are her insides in her?" she asks.

"I think so."

"They're pickled in formaldehyde," Lou says. Lou is still looking out the window. Their father has just accepted a flask from the reporter, and now he's shaking the reporter's hand. "What a prick," Lou says.

Norma sighs. She walks over to a chair and drops into it and removes her glasses, which have felt too tight ever since they fell into the eavestrough. She knows that the prick Lou is referring to isn't one of the newspapermen, it's their father. Lou says she hates their father. Norma's never been able to hate him and especially couldn't now, when he's so pathetic. Even Lou has to admit that he loved their mother. What drove their mother to drink and probably to the roof, and what drove him, part way at least, to every bad, crazy thing he did, never really drove the two of them apart. Yesterday, in their mother's bedside table, Norma found the kidney stone that he gave their mother—for luck and instead of an engagement ring—on the night they met. Lou wouldn't look at it. Lou blames him.

Lou turns from the window. Norma is staring at her without glasses. Sandy is crying quietly, leaning into the casket. She seems to be stroking their mother's face.

"What are you doing?" Lou asks her.

"Changing her lipstick," Sandy sobs.

Lou feels nauseated. "I need some air," she says and leaves the room.

Going around a corner in the hall, she bumps into their father.

"Oh, hi!" he says, astonished.

His whiskey breath makes her stomach heave. "The last room on the left," she says, shoving by him.

She opens an Exit door and is in the parking lot. The heat slams into her. The photographer is gone, but the reporter is still there, resting against a car that's in the shade. He gets up and wanders over.

"What are you hanging around for?" she asks.

"Waiting for you." He lights her cigarette. The back of his hands and forearms have a rug of black hair on them. "So," he says, "was it an accident or what?"

"Didn't the whiskey loosen my father's tongue?" she asks sarcastically.

"I'd like to hear what you've got to say."

She wonders why she doesn't tell him. It's none of his business, but that's not the reason.

"Off the record," he says. "Strictly between you and I."

"Between you and *me,*" she corrects him.

He dips his head to look in her face. He has whiskey breath, too.

"I've got to go back in," she says, tossing away most of her cigarette.

"Hey, come on." He grabs her arm.

"Let go."

"One minute, okay?"

"FUCK OFF, OKAY?"

They stare at each other. He drops his hand.

In the washroom she looks for feet under the cubicle doors. Sees none. She shuts herself in a cubicle and starts crying. She can't believe it, it makes her mad, because last night she imagined she experienced the final evolution of her heart.

What is she crying about? Not about their mother or about the baby that she cried at the thought of having and still wouldn't keep. She isn't crying for these deaths on either side of her.

She's crying because. . . . She doesn't know why. But when she's cried herself out, the relief leaves her light-headed. No, it's more than relief—it's the same feeling she had up on the roof with their mother and Norma (although she never felt more separate from everyone), when she was above the whole subdivision, and the clouds rolling from horizon to horizon made her think of a great migration. The wind whipped her hair. It was warm and windy. Not dark or light. Their father couldn't get to her. He couldn't climb the ladder! Their mother wouldn't climb down. There was a standoff, a stopping of time. Something was going to happen—Lou felt that much, although she didn't know it was going to be something so terrible—but in that suspended minute or two, Lou was in heaven, on the verge of flying even. Doing out of no fear what their mother, a few seconds later, did terrified.

CHRISTMAS

1959

Between opening gifts and having breakfast, their father always got out his Bible and read from St. Luke, Chapter 2. For some reason their mother left the room at this point, and although on Christmas Day 1959 the girls found out why she did, they were still pretty young then (Sandy eight, Lou nine, Norma ten). There were years to go before they saw the link between their own baby brother and their mother's aversion to the mention of babies, including the baby Jesus.

Without fearing God (how many times had she dared him to strike her dead, show his face, burn a bush?), Lou was the one who remembered and pondered the Bible stories, and at night in bed she sometimes retold them to her sisters, who consequently thought, as she did, that Jesus died in Calgary, where the cowboys were now. They associated this with his birth in a small barn and thought that in spite of having to die nailed to a cross, he was incredibly lucky, not just to be born among the animals but to have adults kneeling before him and giving him precious gifts. You only got this kind of treatment, Lou informed her sisters, if your father didn't plant a seed in your mother—if your father didn't have anything to do with you getting made.

No seed also meant that your mother was pure, like a pure blue sky or pure gold. The girls equated the Virgin Mary's purity with soft, flawless, hollow, crystal-clear beauty. They loved her because of her purity and because she was like their mother—meek and mild, named Mary, and different from all other mothers.

Instead of doing housework all day and going outside now and then to shop or sweep the porch, their mother went outside once a year. The rest of the time, from six in the morning until eleven at night, she watched TV. Only in the fall, after Aunt Betty had dropped off cousin Mary Jane's old clothes, did she do anything else. The girls would come home from school and hear the sewing machine humming in the basement. "What are you making?" they'd cry, running down to her. "Ask me no questions, I'll tell you no lies" was their mother's answer. She worked fast, broke thread with her teeth. Her hands were steady. In no time there'd be a new dress for each of them.

Sometimes these sewing fits inspired her to other activity. "Lou," she'd say, "go out and buy me a bag of cooking apples." Then she'd bake a pie. She knew how to tap-dance, and if they begged her, and their father wasn't home yet, she might get her tap shoes from the trunk and click out "Tea for Two."

Christmas Day was the one time she went out of the house. After breakfast she put on her girdle, her black slip, her black dress with the tiny red and blue flowers, new nylon stockings that their father would bring home the day before, shiny black high heels, and the tomato-red lipstick she used to wear on stage during her hoofer days. Sandy—who was her image, who was so golden and fragile that women in the street threatened in longing voices to steal her—fell into rapture watching their mother dress. Each year she saved the piece of toilet paper their mother smacked between her lips; she sniffed the lipstick scent and kissed the lonely, floating mouth, then put it in her own white-covered Bible, between two pages of all red words, which was Jesus speaking. So far she had three of their mother's mouths in there.

They were, all of them, in their best clothes for going to Uncle Eugene's and Aunt Betty's. Taking the show on the road, their mother called it. Their father's nerves were always shot driving there. He chain-smoked, yelled at them in the back seat to shut up. This year he almost drove into a stopped truck and killed them all without even noticing. Over the screech of his brakes he was asking their mother for the tenth time if she thought Mary Jane would like Cindy the Mardi Gras Doll.

"She'll dance with joy," their mother said.

He shook his head. "What the hell," he said. "The whole goddamned business has gotten out of hand."

Lou muttered, "Who does he think fat Mary Jane is, anyway? The Queen?" But she knew (their mother told them last year) that it wasn't the gift he bought for Mary Jane that got him worked up every Christmas, it was Uncle Eugene being a rich bank president and driving an Oldsmobile, though he was the younger brother and only named after the man who wrote "Wynken, Blynken and Nod," while their father, the older brother and named James Agar Field after a president of the United States, sold used cars and drove their old Packard. "Brotherly rivalry," their mother explained. "Such as Cain and Abel had."

It turned out that Mary Jane already had a Cindy the Mardi Gras Doll. She dropped the one they gave her back in the box, where it landed upside down with its taffeta underpants showing. Their father pulled out his wallet and tried to give Uncle Eugene money. "Buy her whatever she wants," he said. "The biggest doll in the store."

"I've got the biggest doll," Mary Jane said stonily.

From Aunt Betty and Uncle Eugene the three sisters each received what seemed to them an amazing new invention—white roller skates that laced up like ice skates.

"Top of the line," Uncle Eugene said to their father. "Straight from Germany." He told Sandy to come over and give her old Uncle Eugene a big kiss, but she kissed Aunt Betty's soft, powder-smelling cheek instead, and Aunt Betty hugged her too hard and screamed, "Oh, my little beauty!"

"Mary Jane!" Uncle Eugene yelled. "Go show your cousins what you got."

"Come on," Mary Jane said, leaving the room. Their mother stood up to get lost in the crowd as far as the kitchen, but Aunt Betty screamed at her to sit down, she'd get her a drink.

"Ginger ale," their mother said, handing over her glass.

"That'll be the frosty Friday," Aunt Betty cried.

Mary Jane led the way down the long hall, swivelling her body to show off the bouncy fullness of her skirt and to remind them that she was the oldest and that in her house she could walk however she wanted to. "Wait 'til you see," she said.

"What is it?" Sandy asked.

"Just wait."

It was a Mary Jane doll. Standing in the middle of the room, its arms bent up in an "I surrender" pose. It was the big doll that Mary Jane spoke of earlier. Incredibly, it's face was Mary Jane's ugly face, and it was as fat as she was. A fat, ugly doll wearing Mary Jane's pink chiffon dress and pink bow in its tightly curled brown hair, and even wearing Mary Jane's pointy, pink glasses.

Mary Jane strutted over to it and in an exasperated, motherly manner straightened its bow. A man who owned a doll factory made it, she said, from pictures Aunt Betty gave him. Just its head cost a hundred dollars.

"What's her name?" Sandy whispered. She had a pain in her throat. "Is it Mary Jane?"

"No. It's Annette."

"Annette Funicello?"

"Annette Funicello Field."

Sandy went around behind the doll, and that was better, not seeing the face. With the very tips of her fingers she touched its hair.

"Careful," Mary Jane scolded. "Her head's breakable."

Sandy quickly dropped her hand. Naturally she was jealous, but what had her on the verge of tears was the doll's ugliness (for even at eight years old Sandy was an aesthete), and more crushing still, the realization that Aunt Betty, whom she had always envisioned wishing upon a star for a beautiful daughter, wanted more Mary Janes, wanted Mary Jane to have a sister, or a baby . . . whatever a doll this big was.

Norma said, generously, "It's neat," although she didn't play with dolls and couldn't imagine how her cousin was anything but tortured by this one. Norma gave the doll another glance and felt herself blush. Everyone said that Norma and Mary Jane were the ones who looked like sisters.

"It's *fat,*" Lou said. She pulled up the doll's dress. "Big fat bum," she sang. "Big fat bum."

"Leave her alone," Mary Jane screamed. "I'm telling."

"Oh, who cares," Lou said, falling on the pink wall-to-wall carpet.

Mary Jane fussed with Annette's bow. "I know something that you don't know," she sang.

Sandy asked, "Is it about Annette Funicello Field?" She couldn't resist lowering one of the doll's arms and sliding her finger into its curled-up hand. What if the hand squeezed hers? She would scream.

Mary Jane didn't answer. She just kept singing that she knew something they didn't know, until Lou twisted her arm behind her back and ordered her to tell.

"Okay," Mary Jane said, not putting up a fight. "Just remember, you made me."

They went down the basement to Uncle Eugene's workroom. When they were all inside, Mary Jane shut the door behind them and pulled the string on the light bulb that was hung down on a wire. Uncle Eugene's tools were in a mess on the bench. Where they belonged on the wall, he had painted their outlines in white. Norma said. "That's what they do around your body when you get murdered on the street."

"Hey!" Lou yelled. "Aunt Betty! Ha ha. Va-va-va-voom!" She pointed at a calendar that had a color picture above it of a strange lady, with gigantic bare breasts, sitting with her legs crossed on top of a ladder, filing her nails with a saw.

"Found it," Mary Jane said, lifting a small metal box out from behind a stack of planks.

"So, big deal," Lou said. "What's in it?"

Norma asked, "Is it a dead man's hand?"

"You'd never believe it in a million years if I told you." Mary Jane lifted the box up onto a chair and opened the lid.

Papers, letters inside. That's all.

Lou shoved Mary Jane. "Let's see."

"Quit it!" Mary Jane said in a furious voice. She rifled down through the pile, and near the bottom pulled out a paper. A piece of folded-up old newspaper. She slammed down the lid and opened the paper on it.

"Read that!" she screamed at Lou. "You just read that, big smarty pants. I hate you!"

Norma had a premonition. Inside her head there was a cold light that she knew was God's warning, but she read too, over Lou's shoulder. "Monday, May thirty-first, nineteen forty-eight," Norma read out loud. "Gee, before we were even born."

Lou pulled the paper closer. "Is that Mommy?" she said. "That's Mommy."

"That's your mother!" Mary Jane cried.

"Let me see!" Sandy cried, squeezing between her big sisters.

There was a photograph of their mother in a dark suit and in a hat that had a little white feather sticking out of it. She looked surprised. Behind her was their father's face, looking mad and too young to be their father.

Norma started to read the headline out loud: "No changes—"

"*Charges,*" Lou interrupted. "No charges laid—"

"—in Niagara Falls baby death," Norma and Lou read together.

Norma looked up at their cousin. Mary Jane's cheeks were apple red, the same as her doll's. "Read it!" Mary Jane cried.

"Tray—" Lou said, going on to the subheading. She nudged Norma. "What's this word?"

"Tragic," Norma said. "Tragic accident, court rules."

Sandy sucked in her breath. "A baby died," she whispered wide-eyed, covering her mouth with her hands.

"You had a brother," Mary Jane burst out. "I knew. I knew before you did!"

"You never did," Sandy said. She stood on her tiptoes to see over Lou's arm. Lou was running a finger under the words as Norma continued to read out loud.

"A Sunday outing . . .," Norma read. Pretending to read along with her, Sandy said, "Outing."

"No whiteness has come forward," Norma read.

"No whiteness," Sandy echoed softly.

"No *witness!*" Mary Jane cried. "Stupid! You can't even read. *I'll* read it."

"Shut up!" Lou cried, giving her cousin a push. "Shut your big fat trap."

Norma went on reading. "He fell out of my arms, Mrs. Field test . . . testif . . . test. . . ."

Sandy murmured, "He fell out of my arms, Mommy said."

"The fate of Baby Jimmy . . .," Norma read.

"Baby Jimmy," Sandy repeated, thinking that this must be their father when he was a baby.

"Read what it says at the end!" Mary Jane cried. Her arm shot by Sandy's face.

"Ow!" Sandy protested. The sequins on Mary Jane's sleeve had scratched her chin.

"See!" Mary Jane cried, stabbing a roly-poly finger at the bottom of the column. "See, it says, 'The ruling came in . . . in spite. . . .'" She clicked her tongue impatiently. "Well, anyway, it says that your mother threw the baby over Niagara Falls. *Threw* him, not dropped him. Because he would have landed on the ground if she just dropped him."

"Liar! Liar!" Lou shouted.

". . . to span the bank," Norma read, "between the wall and the water."

Lou snatched the paper up, and Norma stepped back. On the radio upstairs a man sang, "Chestnuts roasting on an open fire." Norma thought, that's what cowboys would do. She swaggered over to the calendar lady and touched her finger to the nipple of the right breast. She froze, her finger in the air, stunned by her daring.

"You made me show you." Mary Jane sounded frightened.

Lou stared at the picture of their mother and father. It felt like a matter of life or death that she remember if she'd seen that feathered hat before. "Did the baby die?" Sandy asked. Mary Jane tried to take the newspaper back, but Lou crumpled it into a ball.

"You're going to get it!" Mary Jane cried.

Lou hurled the ball at her, marched over to the workbench and picked up the hammer. Mary Jane screamed. Sandy screamed. Up in the living room they thumped on the floor to keep it down. Taking the hammer with her, Lou left the room and went upstairs. She marched right past the living room, through her name thundering out of there. Down the hall to Mary Jane's bedroom.

"Stop!" Annette Funicello's one raised hand said.

Lou windmilled the hammer.

She windmilled the hammer but didn't step any closer to the doll. Already her intention had deflected from that dumb, innocent, one-hundred-dollar breakable head back to the real Mary Jane.

No, back to *him!* (She heard him coming down the hall.)

. . .

Near midnight Sandy tiptoed down to her sisters' bedroom.

She wished that it was she and Norma who shared a room. Norma had a round face with smooth pink half-heart cheeks, and she was big and soft to sit on; she let Sandy sit on her and collapse on her in a game they called Chair. Her voice was low, drifting-off. She never got mad the way Lou did. Lou wasn't even the oldest, but she thought she was the boss when their father wasn't around.

Sandy went over to Norma's bed. "Are you awake?" she whispered.

"Yeah, we can't sleep," Norma said. She and Lou had been telling each other that's why there were no photographs after their mother and father got married, none for three years. And remember before their mother stopped going out for drives, the time they were all in the car, and Lou asked if they could ever go to Niagara Falls, and before their father could speak, their mother made him pull over, and she got out and just walked around in some bushes for about half an hour? Remember seeing her purple pillbox hat (that's all that showed above the bushes) wandering around?

Norma and Lou had been exchanging these revelations and in long stretches of silence waiting for an entire, lasting sensation of what it was like to have a brother who was dead because your mother dropped him.

Norma absolutely exonerated their mother. Having held several babies, she knew how they squirmed in your arms, how easy it would be to drop one. She could just picture it—their mother being distracted by Niagara Falls, not paying attention for a second, crying, "Oh, little Jimmy!" but he was gone, rolling across the bank and over the falls. Did he get all smashed up? Since Norma had never seen a waterfall, she imagined calm water at the bottom. She imagined Jimmy in a knitted white bonnet, doing the dog paddle, and his blanket floating around him like a lily pad.

What if it had been Sandy? On the way back from Uncle Eugene and Aunt Betty's, Norma had this thought and pulled her little sister over to her and held her until they were home.

Another thought that kept crossing Norma's mind was their brother's age: twelve. Twelve in February if he had lived. She figured it out from the date of the newspaper and how old the story said he was when he fell. He would have played with her—catch, football, road hockey. The two of them would have played games girls don't play and boys don't play with her. Twelve. A twelve-year-old brother is what she'd have had now, if their mother hadn't dropped him by accident.

Lou didn't think it was an accident, but she also let their mother off the hook, because who wouldn't have thrown that damn baby? which Lou now envisioned as their father. A baby *him*—the brush cut, the shot nerves. Always bawling. At the same time she was furious with their father for not having saved it. Why didn't he? When he was in the war, he ran from cover and saved a man being shot at. In Mary Jane's bedroom she'd tried to whack him one with the hammer, but before she could, he got it away from her, threw her over his knee and spanked her. Then he dragged her down the hall and ordered her to tell Uncle Eugene and Aunt Betty she was sorry. But by then she was thinking, "I'm a doll" (she had turned herself into a doll), so how could she cry or speak or be bad, let alone be sorry? He spanked her again. He kept spanking her until Uncle Eugene hauled him off into the kitchen, where in a low voice that they nevertheless heard out in the hall, he explained about the newspaper cutting downstairs. Their father said, "Jesus fucking Christ"—on Christmas Day. When he came back out of the kitchen, he stalked over to the closet and began throwing out their coats and mittens and hats. Their mother's pillbox hat rolled down the three stairs into the living room. "Get dressed," he said.

"What about dinner?" Aunt Betty screamed.

In the car Lou tugged the back of their mother's fur collar. She wanted their mother to speak, even if it was only to whisper "Don't," but their mother pretended not to feel anything, and her face in the rearview mirror was dreamy. Lou fell back against the seat. Beside her, Norma and Sandy whispered. Lou looked out her window and let her eyes fill at the unfairness of the spanking and of being the daughter of their father. His tantrums. His yelling and complaining. All his rules. The minute he came back from work, she and Norma and Sandy had better be lined up in the front hall for inspection, or else, and if they didn't pass muster, he ordered them to wash or change on the double. What other father did this? After inspection he went outside and looked up and down the street for something to get in an uproar about: the neighbors' dandelions, their dirty cars, their unshovelled driveways, their noisy kids.

She was glad that the baby of him had died. She knew that their mother threw it. But for some reason she kept her mouth shut the rest of the day, kept it shut even now, talking about it with Norma.

Sandy climbed into Norma's bed, under the covers. She made a slow, unfurling motion with her arms. "Mommy *threw* our brother over Niagara Falls," she said wistfully.

"*Dropped* him over," Norma said.

"It was a tragic accident," Lou snapped from the next bed. She didn't want the damn kid to start crying and get them in trouble.

"Can you tell us a story?" Sandy asked her.

"What about?"

"About David."

Lou sighed. "Oh, okay." She waited until her sisters had climbed into her bed, one on either side of her. "It came to pass," she said in her quiet, expressive storytelling voice, "that a woman had a boy child that she wanted to save from being murdered by the king, so she covered him with slime and put him in a basket amongst the bulrushes."

"No, that's Moses," Sandy said.

"Yeah," Lou said, realizing it was. "I know."

Sandy woke up first. She was curled into Norma's stomach and looking straight at Lou's face, which had a peaceful aspect that Sandy had never seen when Lou was awake. Eight years later, lying on a vibrating bed in the middle of twin brothers, Sandy would open her eyes from a dream that she wasn't sleeping between those brothers but between her sisters. "It's not nymphomania!" she would declare and then cry her heart out with relief and for old times.

Now, very gently, she braided a lock of Lou's long dark hair around her own wrist. She made a Lou-hair bracelet. She was very quiet and gentle, but Lou woke up anyway and said, "The TV's not on." Sandy shook off the bracelet. "Something's the matter," Lou said, jumping out of bed and running down the hall to their parents' bedroom.

Their father was standing at the window, reading the thermometer. "Well, your mother's gone and gotten herself the flu," he said, as if that didn't take the cake.

Norma and Sandy came into the room and went over to stand beside Lou, who was feeling their mother's forehead. Their mother was asleep on her back, all the blankets thrown off.

"She's burning up," Lou whispered.

"Even her hand," Norma whispered, stroking it.

Sandy felt the other hand, the tapered fingers that were smooth and ladylike from no work. "We're sorry," she whispered. She assumed that their mother's fever was caused by them finding out about their brother.

The rest of the day, although he was home, their father had them doing the checking-up on her. "When you're straight commission, you can't afford to get sick," he said. She never really woke up. They didn't think about taking her to the bathroom, and sometime after lunch she wet the bed. Then their father was forced to come in and carry her out into the hall, where he changed her nightgown while Norma and Lou changed the sheets. That night he slept on the chesterfield.

The next morning she was awake when they went in to see her. She didn't speak, but she looked at each of them in turn as if she had something important to say. "What?" they urged her. They brought her a bowl of Frosted Flakes and tried to feed her, but she wouldn't chew or even swallow until Lou got the idea of putting a plastic Flav-R straw in her mouth. After she had sipped up all the milk in the bowl, they walked her to the bathroom, Lou supporting her on one side and Norma on the other. Lou and Norma rubbed deodorant under her arms on top of her nightgown and brushed her teeth as she sat on the toilet, and Sandy combed her long, wavy hair that was as golden as her own, that she twined with her own to enjoy the likeness. All the while they asked her if she was all right and begged her to answer, but she could hardly keep her eyes open.

"Shovel those liquids into her," their father ordered when he phoned from work. He suggested soup, Postum, evaporated milk, juice. Any liquid in the house except for her "coffee."

For six days she was the same. Sleeping most of the time, feverish, thrashing, incoherent. Obviously upset. "I wonder what she's dreaming about?" Norma said.

"Television shows," Lou decided. "All mixed up together. Hoss and Lassie and the Beaver."

"Yeah," Norma said. "And they're all fighting, and the show never ends."

It didn't occur to the girls that their mother should have a visit from a doctor. Nobody who wasn't related to them ever visited. Aunt Betty phoned once, to see if everyone had recovered from Christmas, and Norma told her that their mother had the flu, but she never thought to ask for help. She and Lou did everything around the house anyway. The only job Sandy did was the mending. That started one day when, without being asked, she sewed patches on the worn-through elbows of their father's red flannel shirt. It turned out that she could darn, too. She had their mother's talent that way. The fact that she was a miniature of their mother meant that this was no big marvel. It also meant that nobody pressed other chores on her—nobody imagined that she might be good for anything else.

"How's the food situation?" Aunt Betty asked.

"We're running out of stuff for Mommy to drink," Norma admitted.

"Well, *there's* a blessing in disguise!" Aunt Betty screamed.

In fact, it wasn't just juice and soup and milk that they were out of, it was almost everything. Lou phoned their father to tell him, and he dropped by on his lunch hour with some grocery money.

Usually Lou didn't mind doing the shopping. It got her out of the house, and she always picked up a few chocolate bars for herself. But she minded today. She was worried about being away in case their mother died or had to go to the bathroom. And there had been a snowstorm and then freezing rain, so that coming home, it took all her strength to pull the loaded wagon across the shopping-center parking lot, over bumps where tire tracks had frozen in the snow. Halfway across she had to stop and rest on the running board of a truck.

"I've got too many jobs," she said to herself. "I'm carrying too much on my shoulders."

She decided that she didn't give a damn what was happening at home, she was going to sit here for a few minutes. She took out one of her Mars Bars, and as she was ripping off the wrapper, she noticed a boy who was crossing the road, walking right out into traffic and holding up his hand for the cars to brake. He started coming toward her, and then she recognized him. Lance Nipper. The boy with the metal plate in his head.

She watched him closely. He was as unpredictable as a police dog. The plate was supposed to make him normal after he got a head injury in a car accident, but instead it made him different, a loner without fear, and it left him crazy for other metal things—nails and screws that he carried in his pockets; even knives and guns, somebody said.

When he was only a few feet away, he gave her a glance. He would have kept walking.

But she had a compulsion to stop him. His dangerous glance struck her as a dare, and she was in no mood right at that minute to back down.

"Hi," she said.

He halted, looked at her. "Gimme a bite," he said.

"You can have a whole one," she said, standing up and pulling another chocolate bar out of a shopping bag.

He took it and tore the wrapper off with his teeth. There were bits of black hair on his upper lip and chin, like you'd draw them on a jailbird. He *was* a jailbird; he'd been to reform school for stealing a car and driving it to the airport.

"You're Field or something," he said.

"Yeah. Lou Field." How did he know her? she wondered, thrilling. He was in grade seven, three years ahead of her. He'd failed twice anyway. "You're Lance Nipper," she said. She watched him eat, surprised at how handsome his head was close up. She couldn't see any scars or lumps. She'd expected him to have a bit of a ridge where the plate went in. The only noticeable side effect was how his black hair shone blue, like black comic-book hair.

"What'd you buy?" he asked.

"Oh, just groceries." Out of habit, forgetting it was true, she added, "My mother's sick."

He crumpled up his wrapper and shoved it in the truck's tailpipe. "Maybe I'll come to your house," he said.

"No!" she said quickly. "You can't because of my mother." What she meant was because of their father. Their father knew about Lance, said he was the garbage you got in the subdivision when you let apartments go up. If their father found out that Lance had even stepped on their property, he'd call the police.

"No big deal," Lance said. "You come to my place."

"When?"

"Now."

"But my groceries."

"Bring 'em along."

She looked at the bulky paper bags leaning against each other in her old red wagon. She was more inclined to ditch them, along with every other dissuasion.

It was as if she were hypnotized. Magnetized. Trying to keep up with him, pulling along the wagon after all, she imagined she felt his metal plate tugging at the zipper on her jacket and the buckles on her boots. He jingled the screws and nails in his pockets. From the back he looked like a short man.

In the lobby of his apartment building he lifted the intercom phone and punched one of the buttons. "Lemme in," he said.

There was a loud buzzing. As he opened the door, he told her to leave the wagon, but she worried about her groceries being stolen. He motioned her over, and while she held the door ajar, he drew a couple of nails out of his jeans pocket and stuck them through the tops of two bags. "Nobody'll take your groceries now," he said. Nails and screws in unlikely places were his calling card.

She hesitated. "Not everyone knows what they mean," she said.

"Anybody who'd steal your groceries knows," he said.

His mother was in curlers, lying on the chesterfield and watching TV. She didn't look up at them coming into the apartment. They went down the hall to a closed door with a Keep Out sign beneath a drawing of a skull and crossbones that Lou thought she could have drawn way better. When they were both in the room, he reached his arm around her back, and she thought, dizzily, "He's going to kiss me," but he was shutting the door, locking it. There was a hook lock above the handle.

She sat on the edge of his bed. The bedspread had a brick pattern. Brown and red bricks with white mortar oozing out. On the dresser were five big jars with his nails and screws in them, sorted by size.

"How old are ya, anyway?" he asked, leaning against the dresser and unsnapping his jacket.

"Ten," she lied.

"Ya look around eight." He slipped his hand down the back of his blue jeans and pulled out a cigarette that had already been half smoked. From his other back pocket he withdrew a stick match and struck it on his jeans zipper.

"I'm hooked on the damn things," Lou said.

He glanced at her, that glance like the sign on his door, then devoted himself to smoking. He inhaled the way their father did, sucking as if the smoke were stuck halfway down the cigarette. On the TV in the living room a man said, "The wife most likely to be kissed always puts beer on her list."

She was afraid. Not of him, standing there smoking, but of something else, something she couldn't put her finger on. The clock beside the bed said ten after four. Their mother would have needed to go to the bathroom by now. "How about a drag?" she asked.

He came over and held the cigarette to her lips. "Coffin nails," he said, took one last drag himself, then tossed the butt in the wastepaper basket. He lifted a handful of her hair. Dropped it. "I like girls to have long hair," he said. "I like skinny girls." He stayed standing right in front of her, his belt buckle inches from her nose.

"Let's go somewhere," he said.

"Where?" She looked up at his face.

"I've got something to show ya."

Following him down the hall, she did up her jacket and put on her mittens to go outside, but when they got to the bottom of the stairs, he opened a door and went down some more stairs to the basement. In the back of her mind she had some idea that what he was going to show her wasn't an electric train set.

They went halfway along the hall to a metal door. He jiggled the handle.

"Locked," she said.

"To the general public," he sneered, taking a small nail out of his pocket and inserting it in the keyhole.

It was the laundry room. There were two automatic washing machines and two dryers. A green folding table, a pair of sinks and a bulletin board. "So," she said, walking across the room, "what were you going to show me?"

"Ya gotta pull your pants down."

The one note on the bulletin board was for free kittens. None of the telephone numbers was torn off. "What for?" she asked.

"We're gonna play doctor. I'm the doctor, you're the patient."

She turned to face him. "I never had to pull my pants down at the doctor's," she said. But she understood that nothing that had ever happened before counted now.

"Look." He strolled over to her, clinking the nails in his pockets. "It's no big deal. I'll do it if you want. I'll be the patient, you be the doctor."

"No." She shook her head.

He shrugged. "So you be the patient. It's up to you."

Her pants had an elastic waist. She pulled them to her knees, leaving her underpants on.

"All the way down." She pushed them down to her ankles. "I gotta examine ya," he said and told her to go over to the table. With her pants down she walked like a Chinese girl. She was more embarrassed about that than her underpants showing.

He had her bend forward over the edge of the table. Then he yanked down her underpants.

"Don't!" she cried, reaching for them.

He grabbed her wrist, made her let go. He pushed her down on the table. "Ya can't move," he said, sounding mad. She didn't want him to be mad at her.

It seemed like an hour passed. She regarded her hands in their red mittens flat on the table. Her thumb was coming through a hole. She'd better get Sandy to mend that. She listened to him breathing, the only sound.

He touched her. Where she went number two. She flinched, then felt his hand on her bum, pressing her into the table.

"I'm gonna take your temperature," he said. And despite the fact that he was pressing her, she assumed it was over, the most evil thing you could do, the thing she'd come here to do. She'd gone ahead and done it, and it was no big deal. She could pull her pants up, and what he'd do next would concern her mouth. She raised herself a little. As she did, something went up her bum. Cold, thin, smooth. A nail. She screamed.

"Shut up!" His hand covered her mouth. The nail went in farther. Stabbed her. She bit him.

"Shit!" he yelled. The hand flew off her mouth. A red ring of blood on his finger.

She ran to the door, tripping, holding her bum, crying. The nail was still in her. It was like a knife, a knife in her. She pulled it out, screaming.

"What are you howling about? Ya almost bit my goddamn finger off." He was at the sinks, turning on the taps.

She got her pants up, ran to the door, shook the handle. Screamed for help and the police.

"It's open, ya jerk," Lance said.

In the hall there were two exit signs. Which way had they come down? She ran to the left and up stairs that took her straight into the lobby, where the sight of her wagon with the groceries in it was as miraculous as if their mother stood their. Their mother! What time was it? It was dark out. Probably their mother was dead by now.

No! She was better! She was in the kitchen doorway.

"Mommy!" Lou cried, leaving the wagon and groceries in the hall and running to her.

Their mother seized her by the shoulders. "Did you buy my coffee?" Her eyes were on fire. Her hands shook Lou's whole body.

"No," Lou said softly. "No, I can't buy liquor, Mommy."

Their mother let her go and gave a great shudder.

Lou slipped around her into the kitchen. All the cupboard doors were open, and her sisters were sitting on the floor surrounded by cans. "What the hell's going on around here?" she asked.

"We can't find a single bottle," Norma sighed. "Not a single one."

"They're all gone," Sandy said, opening her hands. She didn't like searching anymore—their mother was acting crazy. She wanted their mother to go back to bed.

None of them heard the car pull up. The front door opening hit Lou's wagon, but before their father could get into full swing yelling about that, their mother was in the hall announcing the crisis.

He allowed himself a moment to register her recovery. Then he checked his watch. "Jesus Christ," he said quietly. Lou volunteered that the stores were closed tomorrow, too, for New Year's. She and her sisters had their hands out for inspection, but he didn't give them a glance. He put his arms around their mother and said she should go back to bed. A couple of sleeping pills and she'd sleep right through.

"Run next door," she urged. "Say we're having guests and are caught short."

"I'm not doing that," he said.

"It's Christmas, Jim. Everybody's stocked up."

She was drawing red lines on the back of her hand. Their father snatched what she was doing it with and threw it on the floor. It was a nail, one of the nails Lance had stuck through the shopping bags. Their father declared that she needed Bactine and a bandage on that hand, pronto. He tried to pull her down the hall. "No!" she screamed. She got away from him and threw herself at the door. He booted the wagon out of his way, knocking a bag of cans over, caught her by both arms and turned her to face him. The girls looked on in a calm of horror.

But he didn't hit her. He never had and didn't now. He said, quietly, pleadingly, "For Christ's sake, Mary." Norma would have fallen into his arms. She thought, "He's the only man that goes to church without his wife."

Their mother licked her lips. "It's hot," she rasped. "I can't breathe."

"Do you want a Pepsi?" their father asked brightly. "Lou, go get some." Lou ran to the kitchen.

"No, no, no," their mother groaned. "I've got to go on the roof."

Lou extended the Pepsi bottle.

"Here's some nice cold Pepsi," their father said.

"I'm just going up on the roof," their mother said, nodding that it was okay.

"This'll quench your thirst," their father said heartily.

Lou asked, "What do you want to go on the roof for?"

"I can't breathe," their mother answered, beseeching their father. "I have to be up high. High, high up."

Their father tipped the Pepsi at her lips. Grimacing, she hit it out of his hand. Pepsi splashed on the wall and spilled out a brown lake by their boots.

"That does it," their father said. He scooped their mother up like a bride and began carrying her down the hall to their room. She kicked, thrashed. A pink bow barrette that Sandy had clipped in her hair when she was sleeping shot out. She slapped their father's face so hard his hat fell off.

They heard him drop her on the bed. "Girls!" he shouted. "Get in here!"

He had her on her stomach, her arms pinned behind her back. "Lou, Sandy," he said, "get on the bed, on either side of her." They climbed on. "Okay. Now hold her here." He nodded at her wrists. "Come on." They each held a wrist. Lou could put her fingers right around. "Squeeze," he said. They held tighter. "That's it," he said, letting go, and she jerked, as if she could free herself now, so they held even tighter, they got up on their knees to be stronger, and Sandy sang, "Mommy can't get a-way-ay."

He had Norma sit across her legs. "Now stay put," he ordered. He said he was going to drive to Uncle Eugene's for the whiskey. It would take an hour. He said don't worry, she wouldn't be able to keep on fighting, she was sick. But it was easy to hold her. For a mother she was little.

"Whatever you do," he called from the front door, "don't let her outside."

As soon as he was gone, she stopped struggling. "Get up now," she said in a kind, motherly voice.

"We can't," Sandy said. "You'll go on the roof. You'll fall off." Falling to death was Sandy's biggest fear these days.

Lou asked, "What do you want to go up there for anyway?" She took it for granted there must be a logical reason, such as a bottle stored in the chimney.

"My arms," their mother moaned. She started to cry. Sandy, who was bent over her, looking at her face, instantly let go, and Lou, seeing where Sandy's grip had reddened their mother's thin white arm, said "Oh," remorsefully, and she let go, too.

Their mother reared. Norma tumbled backward, her glasses flying off. In a flash their mother was on her feet. "Stay!" she shouted, holding a hand out like a policeman. They did, they were so overwhelmed by her. But then they heard the front door handle turning, and they tore down the hall after her, catching her before she was out.

"Get away! Let me go!" she screamed. Her eyes threw hatred at them. She was their enemy.

"Let her go!" Sandy cried, starting to hit at her sisters.

"She'll climb on the roof," Norma said. She was pulling their mother's arm. Lou was trying to pin the other one, as their father had done.

"I said let her go!" Sandy screamed, and with both hands she yanked Lou's hair.

"Shit!" Lou yelled. She pushed Sandy as hard as she could, slamming her into the wall.

Norma had her arms around their mother's waist now. Their mother twisted and fought, but Norma was too strong for her. "We need some rope or something," Norma shouted. "We've got to tie her."

"Shut up!" Lou yelled at Sandy howling behind her.

"You get it," Norma shouted at Lou. "I can't see without my glasses. I'll hold her."

Lou ran into the kitchen and down the basement stairs. Where was rope? In their father's workroom? In the laundry room? The clothesline. She tried to pull it down. Then she saw her double-dutch skipping rope on the floor.

By the time she got upstairs, their mother was curled up on the door mat, crying softly. She'd given up. Lou tied the skipping rope around her ankles and wrists anyway, in case. She covered her with her Hudson's Bay blanket from the TV room.

"My mommy," Sandy whimpered like a baby and crawled under the blanket with her. She closed her eyes. Their mother's eyes were closed, but she shuddered and stirred. Norma and Lou stayed beside them, waiting, Lou lying on her back because it hurt up inside her if she sat. Norma found herself sitting on the nail that their father had thrown, and she picked it up and cleaned her fingernails with it, prompting Lou to tell her about the other nail. Regarding her compliance, Lou lied. She said that Lance tied her up—she was tied up today, too, she said.

"Maybe he stabbed an organ or something," Norma whispered, dropping the nail at the thought of where this one might have been.

"Yeah, probably," Lou said distantly.

"If only our brother was alive."

"Don't talk," Lou said. "I'm trying to think." She was thinking of revenge. Setting a fire. Lance and his brick bedspread going up in flames.

"Our brother would have saved you," Norma said quietly. She imagined him appearing in the nick of time, filling the door. Big for his age. Brave, courageous and bold. She imagined him striding home and keeping their mother off the roof with gentle words. What their brother, Jimmy, would have been, she thought, was big and brave and gentle as the lamb of God.

PARADISE

1960

At the beginning of the summer, one evening as the streetlights came on, the girls found a kitten under a bush. Except for a big black spot like a saddle on its back, it was all white—white fur as silky as angel hair.

"Her name shall be Rapunzel," Lou announced, since she'd just read that story.

They carried her home, into the house and down to the TV room, where—a surprising sight—their father was lounging on the couch with his arm around their mother.

"What have you got there?" he asked, grinning.

Their mother said, "A little kitty cat."

"Let's see him," their father said.

Sandy said, "She's a girl."

When they handed Rapunzel to their father, she struggled, but he held her tightly in his big hands, turning her around and lifting up her tail. "She's a girl, all right," he said. "See here?" he said to their mother, pointing under Rapunzel's tail. "This here's a pencil sharpener." He made a whirring noise and pretended he was going to sharpen his finger.

It turned out that the girls didn't need the sales pitch they'd worked out on the way home. "You better tear up some newspapers and make a litter box," was the next thing their father said. Then he put Rapunzel on the window ledge, and she instantly started jumping and clawing at the moths on the other side of the screen.

"No!" Lou scolded, leaping to take her down before their father got mad.

But he held up his hand for Rapunzel to remain on the ledge. "What a card," he said, laughing at her. They all laughed.

For twelve hours they had her. They gave her a bowl of milk and a can of Beefaroni. At bedtime they took her into Norma and Lou's room. All night she was wild, zooming from corner to corner like a beam of light. The girls laughed, then froze, expecting their father to come stomping down the hall. But he never did. Eventually they turned on the bedside lamp, and Sandy dressed Rapunzel in a doll's pink ball gown. They stroked her soft belly. She purred, mewed, batted them, peed in an Easter basket, bit the end of Lou's hair and hung there swinging like a trapeze artist.

In the morning, when their father opened the front door to pick up the newspaper, she ran out into the rain, still wearing the ball gown. Their father wouldn't let them run after her until they'd changed out of their pajamas. "She'll be back," he proclaimed. "Take it from me. Once you feed a cat, you can't get rid of it. I know all about cats. I know everything there is to know about cats."

They left the door open, but she didn't return. When they were dressed, they went out with umbrellas and circled the house, calling her name, hoping she knew it. "Don't worry," their father said, climbing into his car. "She'll be back. I know all about cats."

He started the engine. There was a sound like an electric saw cutting wood. He switched the engine off, opened his door, got out and almost stepped on Rapunzel coming out from under the car, dragging her hindquarters. The skirt of the ball gown was all red. She meowed soundlessly at him and dropped sideways on his left shoe.

Lou decided that night that they had to run away from home. No other response seemed honorable or punishing enough. The next morning, after their father had left for work, she told her sisters the two plans she'd devised. Plan A—walk north through the subdivision to the ravine, where they might find an old boxcar to live in. Eat fish from the river and wild berries. Plan B (in case there were no old boxcars)—take the bus into the city, to the orphanage. Say they've escaped from an uncle who beats them. Pretend that the uncle hitting their heads has made them forget certain things, such as the uncle's name and where they live. Hold out for rich, kind parents.

"Daddy'll find us," Norma said, but not dismissively. Plan A appealed to her, the idea of living in peace in the woods, picking up warnings and pointers from the animals.

"We're going to leave a note behind to foil him," Lou said, clicking open the circular suitcase that their mother had carried around during the war, when she was a dancer in The Light Fantastics. "We're going to say we've gone to Florida." She removed their mother's black tap shoes and packed the plates, forks and spoons and the butcher knife she'd got from the kitchen. Then she packed their underwear. Although it was warm outside, she ordered her sisters to change into their wool slacks and skating sweaters because there wasn't room for winter clothes in the suitcase.

Sandy went into her bedroom and returned in her best dress.

"What's the big idea?" Lou demanded.

"Just to make sure I get adopted," Sandy said, strutting over to the mirror and curling her hair into ringlets around her finger.

Norma said forlornly, "Oh, you'll get snapped up in no time." She pictured mothers pulling at Sandy's arms. She thought that even Lou would probably go fast—to some mother dying to fatten her up. "Let's make a deal," she said. "Okay? We get adopted together, or we don't go. They have to adopt all three of us. Okay?"

"Who will look after Mommy?" Sandy cried, suddenly remembering her.

Lou said, "Don't worry. Daddy will. He likes *her*." She was trying to remember how you told poisonous berries from ones you could eat. She closed the suitcase, opened it again, went back to the kitchen and got five cans and the can opener and packed them. To close the suitcase now, she had to get Norma to sit on it. Next she had Norma and Sandy empty the piggy banks, while she went into their parents' bedroom looking for more money. Four dollars and thirty-five cents in change was in the top drawer of their father's dresser, and she took it and put it, along with the money from the piggy banks, in her black shoulder purse that she used for grocery shopping. Then she wrote the note:

"Dear Daddy. We have gone to Florida because you killed Rapunzel. We are gone forever. If you look for us you will waste your time. From your daughters, Norma, Louise and Sandra."

She laid it on his pillow, on the unmade bed. Never again would she make that damn bed, she thought, feeling as if she were already far away, a lot farther away than she intended to go.

Norma carried the suitcase, Lou carried the purse, and Sandy carried her Miss Flexie Doll. It was a beautiful morning, warm, still, not a cloud in the sky. Between the houses, pale yellow light poured down.

First they went to the cigar store to pick up sunglasses for travelling in disguise. Then they headed north, into a part of the subdivision they'd never walked through before. The streets had names like Deep Pine Woods and Shady Oak Hill, although there were no hills and just a few spindly maple trees held up by sticks, the same as on their street.

Lou tried to keep heading north, but with the streets curling back on themselves and with all the houses looking alike, she wasn't as sure of where she was going as she pretended to be. Kids stared at the three of them in their sunglasses. A boy in a Davy Crockett hat asked, "Are you beatniks?" and about a half hour later, there he was asking it again.

"Oh, no, we're back where we started from," Norma said setting down the suitcase. Her arm was killing her.

Sandy sat on the curb and took off her sunglasses. Since there'd been no children's pairs, she'd got a woman's pair, gold-rimmed ones with red jewels in the corner. The men's ones were cheaper—Lou bought a pair of them—but Sandy would never wear men's. Norma had to wear clip-ons over her real glasses.

"My feet hurt," Sandy said.

"I told you not to wear those damn party shoes," Lou said. "Hey, kid," she said to the boy. "How do you get to the ravine from here?"

"What ravine?"

"Where the trains go through."

"Search me."

"Why don't you just ask him how we get out of here," Norma said, sitting beside Sandy.

"Go that way, then that way, then that way, then that way, then that way," the boy answered, zigzagging his arm.

"I'm thirsty," Sandy whined.

"Shut up," Lou said. "Just everybody shut up and let me think." She was thirsty, too. And boiling hot in her skating sweater, but she couldn't take it off because she didn't have anything on underneath. She stared at the boy, who stared back, obediently quiet. Nothing occurred to her except to go on to Plan B. "Okay, kid," she said. "I'll make you a deal."

For a can of pears he led them back to the shopping center. Sandy took off her shoes and socks and walked on lawns until a bee stung her foot, and then Norma had to carry her piggyback, and Lou had to carry the suitcase.

At the shopping center again they bought three Cokes, some Bactine for Sandy's foot and a purple wax hairband that Sandy would wear for a while and they could all have a piece of later to chew on. But they waited at the bus stop for so long that the hairband melted on Sandy's head. The only way Lou could remove all the wax was to cut off the hair it was stuck to. She used the butcher knife.

"I want to go home," Sandy whimpered.

"Forget it," Lou said. "We're never going back to that dump."

It didn't cross Sandy's mind to go home alone. Clutching her doll, she sat on the suitcase.

"The bus will be along any minute, honey," Norma said. How long had they been waiting? she wondered. An hour? There were no trees. No shade. Only the thin strip that the bus-stop pole made. A lady who'd waited with them for a while and then decided to walk said she bet the bus had overheated and was stalled somewhere. She also told them that about a half hour ago, behind the drugstore, a man collapsed from sunstroke, and the druggist called an ambulance.

Norma saw a piece of cardboard by the curb. She picked it up and brought it over to fan Sandy with. Sandy lowered her head, and on her neck where her hair parted, Norma saw a heat rash. Poor baby, Norma thought. To distract her, she said, "I spy with my little eye, something that is—" She glanced all around for a color. "That is—grey."

"Movie stars," the driver said as they were boarding the bus. They kept forgetting about their sunglasses. When Lou was paying him, she asked if this bus went downtown. He said they'd have to go on the subway, but he'd take them to the station.

They sat on the seat behind him. Norma's legs were dripping perspiration inside her winter slacks. The woman across from her was holding a squirming baby boy, and that made her think of their brother, Jimmy. Sometimes she dreamed about him, of finding him, still a baby, in a carriage on the street. "Why haven't you looked for me?" he asked sadly, and she thought, "Wow! A talking baby!" Another dream she had was that she was playing with a boy who had Lou's thin dark face and who kept trying to kiss her. "It's okay, I'm your brother," he said. But she knew he was lying because their brother would be full of grace.

"I'm too hot," Sandy said softly. She dropped her doll on the bus floor and just sat there, watching it slide as the bus turned.

"Your doll," Norma said, picking it up, and then she saw how pink Sandy's face was. "Lou, look at Sandy," she said, lifting her clip-on glasses.

Lou thought of the man fainting behind the drugstore. "We've got to get her a drink," she said. "We better get off." She rang the bell for the next stop.

The bus driver let them off a block past the stop, where there was a restaurant they could go to. Sandy wouldn't walk, so Norma had to carry her piggyback again. Behind her jewelled sunglasses Sandy closed her eyes.

They sat at the counter and Lou ordered three large Cokes. By the cash register there was a little fan that she turned to blow on Sandy, who lay her head on the empty plate in front of her.

The waitress, a fat, humming woman, asked if Sandy was sleepy.

"No," Lou answered. "She just likes to put her ear on a plate." Which happened to be the truth.

But the waitress looked unconvinced. "That kid should be home in bed," she said.

"Well, we'd like to go home," Lou lied, detecting a soft heart, "but we don't have any money for the subway tickets." She held the straw to Sandy's lips. "Come on, honey," she said lovingly, for the benefit of the waitress. "Drink it. That's it, sweetie pie. That's it, honey."

Sandy listened in drowsy amazement. Right now, she thought, anything I want, Lou will give me. She wondered what she wanted.

"Do you have money to pay for the Cokes?" the waitress asked. Lou shook her head.

Sandy made her decision. She put her lips to Lou's ear. "I want to go to the orphanage now," she whispered. (Sandy would go through life rewarding people for words of love.)

They had a map to the subway, which the waitress, who also gave them seventy-five cents, had drawn on a napkin. Stick to the shady side of the street, she warned, but even there it was sweltering. The heat made everything look like its reflection in a lake. They passed a drugstore, a shoe-repair store, a hardware store—rows of buildings, two and three stories high with people leaning out of the upstairs windows. Poor, sad, foreign people, Norma thought, who couldn't afford to live in the suburbs. She waved up at a baby whose mother waved its hand.

"We're not in a parade," Lou scolded. Now that Sandy was out of danger, Lou was worried again about discovery. She shoved them into a doorway when a blue Packard like their father's drove by. She walked ahead, as the lookout, so she was the first one to see the kitten, sitting in a doorway and washing itself. Except for a big black spot on its back, it was all white.

"Rapunzel!" she cried.

The kitten went still, one hind leg sticking out. Lou ran up to it and kneeled down with her hands reaching. "Rapunzel, it's me," she said. "Lou." The kitten took off.

Crying its name, they chased it around the side of the building, over a stone wall and across a lawn. Lou dropped the napkin. Sandy's sunglasses fell off. Norma, who was carrying everything, couldn't keep up and imagined her sisters disappearing forever, leaving her with no trace except the doll and this suitcase full of their underwear. But in a minute they were running back, calling out of breath, did she see her?

There was no sense running now, since they didn't know where to go. To cool off, they walked through sprinklers. A woman shook a white cloth out of a window, and that caught their eye, the white. They were searching for white. There were white flowers, a white porch chair, white pillars, a man in a white shirt cutting grass. No, he answered Lou, he hadn't seen a white kitten with a black spot on its back.

In the middle of a street with huge trees and no moving cars Lou called a halt.

"It couldn't have been her, anyway," Norma said. As Lou didn't seem that worried about discovery anymore, Norma raised her clip-ons.

"She didn't have the gown on," Sandy pointed out.

"Boy," Norma said, "it sure looked like her, though. Maybe it was her sister."

"It was *her!*" Lou said furiously. "I saw her. I found her. She was my damn cat." She turned away.

Norma snapped the clip-ons down. She had an urge to lay her hand between Lou's shoulder blades, to feel how hard and straight and familiar Lou's thin back was, like the side of their house. Instead she slipped her hand into Sandy's, and Sandy squeezed it. "Are you okay, honey?" Norma asked her, only now thinking that Sandy shouldn't have run right after a heatstroke.

Sandy gave an extreme childish nod. She pointed to a stone building with a turret. "Is that a castle?"

While they'd been chasing the kitten, Norma hadn't paid attention to where they were. Now she saw that the street was paved with red bricks and that the houses were gigantic. "I think it's a mansion," she said. "This must be where rich people live."

"Come on, let's go," Lou muttered. She started walking.

"Shouldn't we go the other way?" Norma asked.

"*This* way!" Lou yelled without stopping. But she wasn't sure. She was mad enough to kill somebody with the butcher knife. "Stupid shitface cat!" she yelled. There was no one to hear. The man cutting the grass was gone, and there weren't any children playing. All the lawns were bare of children and dandelions.

Under the trees it was almost cool. Lou thought that if they didn't find their way out of here by dinner time, they could sleep under one of these gigantic trees. Maybe they'd even hang around for a few months. Beg for scraps from maids, have the parks all to themselves. They'd passed two parks with swings and slides and not one kid. Where were all the people?

Just as she was wondering this, she saw somebody. An old man who looked like Santa Claus in a Hawaiian shirt and Bermuda shorts. He was clipping a hedge. He waved at them, and Sandy waved back.

"Are you running away from home?" he asked in a kind voice when they walked up to him. He smiled over little round glasses.

"Yes," Sandy answered, and her eyes brimmed with tears.

"We're going to visit Florida," Lou said crossly. Sandy shouldn't have told.

"That's a long walk for three little girls."

"We're just walking to the subway," Lou said sarcastically.

The old man winked at Sandy. "I'll bet a drink of cold lemonade would dry up those tears," he said.

Sandy nodded, letting the tears fall.

Norma put the suitcase down. She was thirsty, her arm was sore, her feet hurt because her saddle shoes were too small. But it was up to Lou to decide.

"Do you own that house?" Lou asked the old man, pointing to the white mansion behind him. If he did, if he wasn't just a workman, they'd stop for some lemonade. She wouldn't mind seeing the inside of one of these places.

He said he did. As they walked across his lawn, he took the suitcase from Norma and held Sandy's hand. All around the edge of the lawn were bright flowers like the ones on his shirt. In the middle was a fountain with a statue of a girl pouring water from a jug. Birds flickered in the trees, and there were two orange and green birds—parrots, the girls realized when they were closer—in a cage that hung from the patio roof.

"Naughty!" one of the parrots squawked.

"Does he mean us?" Sandy asked. The old man twinkled.

The kitchen was almost as big as their entire house. It had two double sinks with old-fashioned taps, two stoves, and cupboards with glass doors, like the kitchen in "Leave It to Beaver." The old man let them turn on the taps and open the cupboards. When they asked what the string hanging from the ceiling was for, he said for opening a vent, and he lifted Sandy up onto the counter so that she could pull it. Then he lifted Lou up to pull it, then went to pick up Norma, but she stepped back, thinking she'd be too heavy for him. "No, that's all right," she said. He got her under the arms anyway and swung her up. For an old man he was strong.

He made the lemonade with lemons. They hadn't known you

could do that. Why didn't he buy it in a can? Lou wondered; he could afford to. At home all they had were cans. "Sometimes," she told the old man, "when it's my turn to make dinner and do the dishes, I just open the cans and put them straight on the burners."

"And then you don't have to wash pots," the old man said.

"Yeah, right."

The old man took out four glasses from the cupboard. They were all different sizes, and one had red balloons painted on it.

"Nothing matches here," Lou said. "The houses are all different, and these glasses, and . . ." she looked around, "the windows." She pointed to one with stained-glass panes and then to the circular one over the sink.

"What do you think about that?" the old man asked. He poured out the lemonade.

"It's neat," Lou said sincerely. She took the glass he handed her and was so thirsty she gulped it all down. He poured her another. "Not bad," she said. "A bit sour, though. And you left some seeds in."

He gave them a tour of the rest of his house. "You really live all by yourself?" Lou asked in disbelief. There was so much furniture, so many rooms. He could sleep in a different bedroom every night of the week. In the bedroom where he did sleep, the walls were covered with paintings and drawings of girls who weren't his daughters or his granddaughters, or even anybody he knew. Just pretty girls, he said, like they were.

"Are you a long way from home?" he asked.

"Yes," Norma answered. She told them that they had been walking all day long.

"Your poor little legs must be tired," he said.

"They sure are," Norma said, leaning toward him. Nobody had ever called any part of her "little" before. But then she saw that his eyes had moved to Sandy, and she stood straight and looked out the window, at the fairyland of flowers down there.

"Shall we give your legs a rest?" the old man asked, lifting Sandy up.

They all went downstairs, Sandy sitting in his strong arms as if in a chair. She touched his bushy white beard. There were balls of wax inside his ear, she saw. She thought that his ear was like a pink rose with pollen in it. "Can I call you Grandfather?" she whispered.

"I'd be honored," he said.

In the kitchen, while he made more lemonade, Lou told him the story she'd thought up for the orphanage, about an uncle who beat them. "He whips Sandy with his belt," she elaborated. "With the buckle end."

The old man frowned.

"And sometimes he bites her."

The old man went still, holding the paring knife in midair. Then he cut a lemon in half and asked Sandy if she would like to make the juice.

"Oh, yes, Grandfather," she said, thinking of Heidi learning to milk the cow.

He pulled a chair up for her to stand on and showed her how to twist the lemon half back and forth on the juicer cone. They did it together, her hand on top of his. He had a smooth, round, brown-spotted hand and round fingers like gloves when you blow into them.

"She knows how to sew," Lou said, opening and slamming a cupboard door.

"Does she now," he said.

"And Norma and I know how to do the laundry and ironing and vacuuming and grocery shopping." She gave a sigh of responsibility. "Norma and I, we know how to do pretty well everything."

"Not only are you pretty girls," he said, "but clever girls as well."

"Lou gets all A's in school," Norma contributed. She guessed what Lou was up to, and she supposed spending a while here, maybe having something to eat, would be all right. But she didn't really believe anymore that they could run away for good. Upstairs, when the old man's eyes dropped from her to Sandy, she'd wondered why she ever got her hopes up about anything.

He carried the lemonade outside on a tray. Although Lou put her sunglasses back on, Norma left her clip-ons in her pocket, in case they made her look sneaky. She and Lou sat on the velvet grass in front of the old man's lawn chair, and Sandy sat leaning against his legs. He touched Sandy's hair where Lou had cut it. "What happened there?" he asked.

"Our uncle did that," Lou answered like a shot.

The old man shook his head.

"Grandfather," Sandy said, brushing the white hair on his legs with the tips of her fingers, "can we live here with you?"

"If you like," he said.

Lou jumped to her feet. "Really?"

"We can't have you going back to your uncle, can we?"

"But can we live with you forever?" Lou asked. "For years?"

He spread his hands. "For as long as you want to."

"Gee," Lou said, beaming at him. "That's great. Okay, I'm going to look around." She tore across the lawn and into the house, and Norma stood with the intention of following her, but she couldn't bring herself to leave Sandy and the old man by themselves. She looked at him. He was watching her.

"Why would you want us to stay?" she asked shyly.

"Because you have nowhere to go."

"But I mean why would you want all the trouble and everything of three girls you don't even know living in your house?"

"Because girls are honey in the heart."

His smile was so kind that she felt ashamed. He asked if she would pick some flowers for the empty lemonade pitcher. He handed it to her, holding the bottom as if it were something else. A precious gift.

"Okay," she said gratefully.

The garden surrounded the entire yard, enclosing it like an enchanted moat. Between the high trees sunlight fell in tinselled shafts. The only garden Norma had ever seen like this one was in a book their father had, called *Twenty Years of Composting*. But he never planted anything other than petunias and geraniums. Six red geraniums in a line under the living-room window; ten white and pink petunias, five each, in a pink, white, pink, white line under the kitchen window.

Some fluffy white flowers that looked as though they'd been made from Kleenex caught her eye. Out of politeness she picked the smallest one. Then she glanced over her shoulder to see if the old man was still watching her. He wasn't. He and Sandy were sitting on the grass, Sandy's bare feet in his lap.

He only wanted to get rid of me, Norma thought. From this

distance all she saw was a strange old man. A strange old man who was tickling her sister's toes. Why wasn't he worried about their uncle coming after them? she wondered. She had an awful thought: what if he planned to kidnap them and sell them on the white slave market in Africa?

Keeping her eye on him, she moved down the garden and picked a few daisies and then a purple flower. The perfume here was as strong as a roomful of dressed-up ladies. Had their mother seen the good-bye note? She would drink straight from the bottle. Norma let out a jagged breath. They should never have left. They'd better go home right now.

But when she walked back across the lawn, intending to order Sandy to put her shoes and socks back on, the old man spoke first.

"A remarkable selection," he said. He came to his feet and reached out both hands to receive the pitcher. "Norma," he said, holding up the pitcher with its four measly flowers, "you are an artist. You have the artist's appreciation of what is not there." And then he kissed her forehead.

She was too overwhelmed to speak.

"You know what?" Lou said, coming out of the house as Norma was returning from the vegetable garden. "He doesn't have a TV. No TV! I even went up into the attic and down the basement and looked. You know what else? He doesn't have a radio. And you won't believe it, but I couldn't find a phone either. Boy, there's going to have to be some changes made around here." She picked up a beet from the apple basket Norma was carrying. "What the hell's this?"

"A vegetable. He asked me to dig up some for dinner." She had four beets, a clump of radishes and eight carrots.

"Hey," Lou said, looking across the lawn, "get a load of this."

Norma came around the edge of the patio to see. The old man was on his hands and knees, crawling in circles, Sandy riding on his back. "He thinks she's three or something," Norma said distantly. She looked at Sandy's bare pink foot tickling the old man under his arm, and she felt as if she'd woken up in traffic. She put down the basket of vegetables. "We have to go home," she said.

"No we don't," Lou said.

"Why does he want us here? He must be crazy."

"He likes us. He likes pretty girls."

"I'm not pretty."

Lou paused too long. "You are too," she said.

"We're going home," Norma said. "I'm the oldest and I'm taking us home." She ran onto the lawn. "Sandy!" she called. "We're going home!"

The old man crawled around to face her. Norma wouldn't look at him. "Come on," she said, trying to lift Sandy off his back, "we have to go home now."

"No!" Sandy cried.

"Leave her!" Lou shouted, running up.

"Come *on,*" Norma said, pulling Sandy.

"Don't!" Sandy cried.

"Simmer down now, simmer down," the old man said.

Norma let Sandy go. "We're going to be late for our dinner," she said, keeping her eyes from him.

He said, "But you're having your dinner here."

Norma shook her head. Sandy shook his collar as if it were reins.

"Do you want us to cook dinner?" Lou asked the old man, to change the subject.

Norma said, "We have a father and mother. Our father never hits Sandy. She's the one he never hits." She looked at the old man now, kneeling there. His face was startlingly red, his glasses were falling off. The top of his underpants was showing at his waist. "Fruit of the Loom," she read upside down. She was on the verge of crying.

But he was the one who started crying. A broken moaning that they thought at first was coughing. Sandy climbed off his back and bent down in front of him. "Grandfather?" she inquired. He hung his head like an old horse.

"Now look what you've done," Lou said to Norma. She couldn't have been more disgusted if he'd gone to the bathroom in front of them. She wondered if he was an alcoholic. That was all they needed.

"Grandfather, what's the matter?" Sandy asked.

He shifted into a sitting position and tugged a red handkerchief out of his shorts pocket. Blew his nose. Took off his glasses and wiped his eyes. "Forgive me," he said. "I was so happy, that's all. I was so happy today."

"But I'm not going to go home," Sandy said. "I *told* you." She squeezed his beard and opened her fingers to feel it spring back.

"Yeah," Lou said. She said that they were all going to stay and that Norma had made it up about their parents, that Norma acted mental sometimes.

Norma walked back to the house. "Hello, beautiful!" one of the parrots screamed. She considered calling the police. She wasn't brave enough or traitorous enough to call their father.

The old man got up and walked, bent over, to his chair. With his socks down, Lou saw that there were bulging purple veins twining around his calves. Sandy came and knelt at his feet, and he brought down his hand on the top of her gold head, covering the hair that Lou had cut. A crow lounged like black paper right above the two of them.

"Would you like some booze?" Lou asked him.

But he was asleep. His hand dropped to Sandy's shoulder, where it lay heavily. As Sandy lifted it off, she checked the time on his wristwatch. "A quarter to five," she whispered.

"Wake him up," Lou said. "He's got to cook dinner. I don't know how to cook those damn vegetables."

Sandy gently pumped his arm, saying, "Grandfather." His head fell back.

"Hey, wake up," Lou said. She gave his shoulder a hard shake. "Boy, he's a deep sleeper," she said, looking around and seeing Norma walking toward them from the house.

A few feet from the chair Norma stopped. What told her? The position of his head? The way his arms drooped over the sides of the chair? "Listen for his heart," she said.

Lou frowned. "What do you mean?"

"Do it, okay?"

Lou pressed her ear against his chest. It sounded like underwater.

"I can't hear it," she said, straightening and taking a few steps back, a little repelled by his chicken-gumbo soup smell.

Sandy got up on her knees and roved her ear over the front of his Hawaiian shirt, thinking she heard his heart and then not hearing it. She stood, took off his glasses, pushed up one of his eyelids and screamed to see the white eyeball.

"Shut up," Lou said. She came over and shook him again, causing his head to fall to his chest. Then, remembering from somewhere, she tried to feel a pulse in his wrist. Nothing.

The three of them stood close together, about five feet from the chair. "A dead person," Norma whispered. Her legs went weak, and she grabbed Lou's wrist to steady herself.

Lou gasped. She had been staring at the old man's hand that had squeezed the lemons, and she thought it was *his* hand, suddenly a ghost's, grabbing her. When he swooped her up in the kitchen, it hurt her a little under her arms.

"There's a bad smell," Sandy said. She started to whimper, and a sob jumped into Lou's throat. Don't cry, Lou warned herself. Yesterday their father said, "Two days ago you didn't even know Rapunzel existed. Just pretend it's two days ago." They wrapped Rapunzel in toilet paper and buried her in an old shoe box that Lou had kept in her closet because when she was younger she used to think that the picture on it, of a dancing, glamorous lady with high heels and pin legs, was their mother.

A fly landed on the old man's ear, then burrowed into his beard. "He smells like poo," Sandy whimpered.

"We better bury him," Lou said.

Norma gaped at her. "We can't do that."

"He told us we could stay," Lou said. "Didn't he? So it's our place now. Right? If people come around, we'll say he went on a vacation. We'll just tell them to go to hell."

Sandy screamed. "It moved!" She clutched Norma's arm.

"What?"

"His hand. It moved."

Lou said, "It did not." She smacked Sandy and told her not to be so damn stupid.

"It did so," Sandy said, crying. She couldn't really believe he was dead, since there was no blood. He scared her, though, the way he seemed to be broken. When his head dropped to his chest, she pulled up his other eyelid, and that eye was there, but it was like blue marble, like a toy eye, blind.

She saw his hand twitch again. "He's waking up!" she screamed.

"Shut up," Lou said. "Do you want the whole neighborhood here? Stop crying!" She started to cry herself. She began marching to the other side of the house, to where the garage was. If he had one, she'd get a wheelbarrow and carry him around to the vegetable garden and bury him there.

Norma ran in front of her. "I'm calling the police," she said, holding out her arms. "I'm going next door and calling them if you dare do anything."

Lou stopped. "You idiot," she said, swiping at her tears, enraged that Norma saw them, "they'll think we did it."

"No, they won't," Norma said. But what if they did? She dropped her arms.

"Bury him!" Sandy screamed.

"SHUT UP!" Lou hollered.

"Let's just go," Norma said. "Okay? Let's just go home and leave him here. Somebody'll find him."

"I'm not going home," Lou said.

"Well," Norma said, "I am."

They stood there looking at each other until Lou turned away. Tears streamed down her face.

"Where's the purse?" Norma asked. She saw it behind the old man. Taking a wide circle around him, she walked over and picked it up, stepping back to open it and count the money. Three times she dropped change because her hands were shaking. There was plenty of money for the subway and buses, she decided, but where was the subway? Where *were* they?

She went into the house to get the suitcase and Sandy's doll. Sandy followed her, saying she had to go to the bathroom. They used the downstairs toilet, and while Norma was going, she warned Sandy never to tell anyone about the old man dying. If anyone found out, she said, they'd all go to jail for murder.

"I couldn't tell *any*way," Sandy said, opening her hands, thinking with a melting heart of the dolls she'd left lined up on her bed with a promise to telephone. "We didn't know what his name was."

Lou had stolen a ten-dollar bill from the pocket of one of the old man's jackets, and this allowed them to take a cab once they were finally on a main street. Norma and Sandy climbed in the back seat and slid over for Lou, but Lou got in the front with the driver, then ignored him, so Norma had to give the address.

When they pulled up in the driveway, their father's car wasn't there. They went inside and down to the TV room, and their mother just said "Hi," as if they had made her lunch and dinner. Their father had to work late, she said, her eyes returning to the screen.

The note was still on his unmade bed. Lou picked it up and read it with a feeling of suspense because she couldn't remember what she'd written and with a feeling of desolation because she remembered how excited she had felt writing it.

"Dear Daddy. We have gone to Florida because you killed Rapunzel." But she doubted now that he'd believe it, because he didn't really kill Rapunzel, not on purpose, anyway. He wouldn't believe that they'd run so far away over something that wasn't his fault.

She crumbled the letter, threw it in the wastepaper basket and started making the bed. What if, she wondered, she'd written, "We have gone to Florida because it hardly ever rains there. Not like here. Cats don't have to climb into car motors to keep warm in Florida."

He'd probably believe a note like that. He'd like a note that blamed the cold weather, which he hated, instead of blaming him. He might even let them go. She could picture him saying, "What the hell. They've got a point."

Not that it made any difference now.

DISNEYLAND

1961

Christmas morning there was only one gift under the tree for each of them. Ugly green pedal pushers with the "sale item" tags still on for Norma and Lou, and for Sandy, a beatnik doll with a string in its back that you pulled to make it talk. Their father let them be miserable for a while, and then he sprang the surprise. He was going to take them to Disneyland in a top-of-the-line trailer that slept five.

"When, Daddy? When?" the girls cried.

He pulled the string on Sandy's beatnik doll. "I'm hip, like, uh, you know, beatnik," the doll said.

"This summer," their father answered. "So for the next six months, thrift is the watchword."

In January air-raid drills started at school for when the Russians dropped the bomb. The principal made a speech in the gymnasium. If it ever suddenly got very light, he said, like a huge flashbulb going off in the sky, you were to cover your eyes with your hands and crouch under your desks until the teacher said it was safe to come out. Then, two by two, you were to file down to the cellar. You were not to try to run home.

"The hell with that," their father said when they told him. "You run home." In spite of the watchword being thrift, he had decided to build a fallout shelter. He had a pamphlet that he'd sent away for called "Pioneers of Self-Defence," all about how to do it.

As soon as the ground was soft enough, around the end of April, he hired a man with a bulldozer to dig a big hole in the back yard. The next day another man in a truck delivered a pile of concrete blocks and some pipes and boards and sheets of metal, and their father went right to work.

It took a month. Every minute that their father wasn't sleeping or working, he was down in that hole. He even ate his meals there. He let Norma help, and she got pretty good at mixing mortar and hammering nails, as long as he didn't yell at her that she was doing it all wrong, which, if he stood over her shoulder, she did. In the morning she woke up yearning for the feel of the hammer in her hand; all day at school she dreamed about hammering. She wished she could do it when he wasn't around, and yet sometimes, when he wasn't mad or tired, she liked the fact that they worked as a team: she mixing the mortar, he setting the blocks; he sawing the boards, she nailing them down. He had to have everything perfect, and the longer she helped him, the more she wanted everything to be perfect, too, the more she couldn't blame him for his tantrums. She wondered if he wished he had a son—Jimmy (who would have been thirteen by now)—to help instead of her.

When the outside was done, the man came back with the bulldozer to shovel the earth back on the roof. Inside, Norma and their father built shelves and fold-up bunks and painted the walls canary yellow, which was supposed to add a note of cheerfulness. Even though Norma said that they never played hopscotch anymore, their father painted a hopscotch on the floor, as recommended by the pamphlet.

He bought two weeks' worth of canned food, jugs for the water, candles, lanterns, paper plates, a chemical toilet, canned heat, a fire extinguisher, a camping stove, and a bow and arrow for hunting game when the bullets ran out. The rest of what the pamphlet said he should buy—bedding, Band-Aids, a transistor radio, a flashlight, batteries, board games, a shovel in case they had to dig themselves out from the house falling on top of them—they already had. A small library of books on nature and American history would prove useful and inspirational, the pamphlet said, but he said, did they know how much a book cost nowadays? and he carried down a box of his old *Life* magazines. He also brought down his World War II gun and three cases of their mother's whiskey.

Every Monday and Friday the girls had to empty the water jugs and refill them with a fresh supply. They didn't mind this chore.

It was small payment for the notoriety and security of being the safest children in the subdivision. Their friends begged to be able to come in when the bomb dropped, and Sandy said "Sure" to whoever asked her. Norma, understanding just how strictly the shelter was designed for a maximum of five people, said she didn't think so—at first she always said that—but she ended up saying, "Oh, all right," because how could she leave her friends to die? "Cash in advance," Lou said. By the end of the school year Lou had made three bucks.

Their father started to have drills, which were nothing like the ones they'd had at school, where the most important rule was to stay calm. He would blow a whistle, sometimes in the middle of the night, and the girls had to run like crazy to do their assigned tasks: Norma, shut and latch the windows and lock the front door; Lou, pull off the electricity switch and turn off the valve to the water heater; Sandy, shut off the furnace switch. The next morning their mother always claimed she'd slept right through, despite the fact that he went on blowing the whistle and shouting "Move it!" until they were lined up in front of the shelter hatch. Down inside he shone the flashlight on his stopwatch and announced how long it had taken. He shone the light in their faces and told them how they could shave off those precious seconds.

He slept down there. He put in an electric outlet so that he could listen to his Judy Garland records. The girls imagined him dancing with the shovel, smooching it: "How's about a little kiss, baby." They loved him being out of the house in the evenings, because they could change the channels, say whatever they felt like and go to bed late. As long as their mother's mug was filled with whiskey, and the TV was on, she didn't care what happened.

The Saturday before the last week of school their father announced that they were going down into the bomb shelter for two weeks. All of them, including their mother.

The girls didn't get it. Did he mean have a drill every day for two weeks? No, he meant stay down for two weeks. Sleep there? they asked. Sleep there, he said, eat there, not come out for two whole weeks.

"Oh, my lord," their mother said quietly.

"Watch TV down there?" Norma asked.

"No TV. We'll be living as if the bomb's dropped and all electricity is out."

Sandy wanted to know what if the phone rang?

"We'll tell everyone where we are beforehand."

"But won't you have to go to work?"

"Nope. I've got two weeks coming."

They still didn't get it. "Two *more* weeks, Daddy?" Norma said.

"Alrighty," he said, clapping his hands, "we'll be going down a week from today. So this Friday I want the sheets and blankets out on the line for an airing. I want the water changed. I want you all to have baths."

"But when are we going to Disneyland, then?" Lou asked.

"We're not," he said.

They weren't down in the shelter an hour when Norma got her first period. Thinking the cramps were from gas, she went into the little closet bathroom and sat on the toilet.

A few seconds later she called Lou in. "I'm dying," she whispered, touching the blood in the crotch of her underpants and holding her finger toward the lantern.

"You moron," Lou whispered. "It's the curse."

"How do you know?"

"Well, what else? What a goddamn moron."

"Do you have it?"

"No," Lou said, as if she wouldn't be caught dead.

Norma looked at the dark stain on her underpants. She was dripping blood into the toilet now. "What am I going to do?"

"Use Kotex. But I guess there isn't any down here." She scanned the shelf beside the toilet. Band-Aids, toilet paper, Tums. "I know there's some in Mommy's closet, because I just bought her a box." She opened the door. "Mommy? Can you come here?"

"What's going on?" their father asked.

"Nothing. Mommy?"

Their mother's slippers flapped as she crossed the floor.

"Norma's menstruating," Lou whispered to her.

Their mother covered her mouth with both hands.

"Do we have any Kotex down here?" Lou asked.

"Jim," their mother said, turning around. "Lou just has to scoot up to the house for a sec."

"What the hell are you talking about?" he yelled. "There's radiation out there."

"Well, there isn't really, Jim."

"Yeah, but we have to act like there is, or we ruin the whole exercise."

"Norma has become a woman."

Silence. Norma shut her eyes.

"What the hell are you talking about?" their father asked again.

Their mother said, very distinctly, "Ruby Keeler," which must have been a code name, because their father said, "Jesus Christ."

"So Lou just has to scoot up and bring down some napkins," their mother said.

"She's really bleeding?" he said.

"Well, yes, Jim."

"Alrighty. We tear up a sheet." He grabbed a green-striped flannelette sheet from the shelf where the linen was and ripped it in half. "What do ya think the pioneers did?" he asked.

For the rest of the morning Norma was allowed to lie on the bunk with their mother, who read the *TV Guide*, smoked cigarettes and sipped whiskey from her coffee mug. When their father wasn't looking, she let Norma have a sip to ease her cramps.

Lou and Sandy had to stick to The Regime. This was a chart that their father had written out on a piece of yellow Bristol board and nailed to the wall. Down one side was the time of day, and down the other was what they were supposed to do at that time. "Eight o'clock—rise; eight o'clock to eight-fifteen—use toilet in the following order: Dad, Sandy, Norma, Lou, Mom." Et cetera. In front of some of the events were the initials "l.o.," standing for "lights out" to save on candles and fuel. For instance, the singsong and afternoon exercises had an l.o. in front of them.

Ten-thirty to eleven-thirty in the morning was exercises with the lights on. For the first part their father led Lou and Sandy in a march round and round the shelter, hollering, "Hup two three four! Left!

Left!" Next was touching toes twenty-five times, and after that was twenty-five push-ups. The floor was cold on their hands, and Lou and Sandy could only do a couple of push-ups before their arms gave out.

"Five! Six! Seven!" their father went on counting. Between each of his push-ups he clapped, holding himself in the air for a second. He glared out of the corner of his eye for them to keep on going, and they managed to do a few more, but it was just too hard.

He did fifty. Then he bounced up like a jack-in-the-box and shouted, "Stride jumps!"

They jumped facing him, stepping on each other's toes and hitting each other's hands because there wasn't enough room. His mouth was open in a circle that gusted coffee-smelling breath at them. Sweat streamed down his face. If they'd seen a man on the street looking like he did, they'd have run away.

"Okay, play hopscotch," he said after the stride jumps.

"We need stones," Lou said.

"Play without 'em." He cranked the blower for air, then poured himself a glass of water. Lou asked if she could have one.

"Wait 'til lunch," he said. "We have to ration."

"Psst." It was their mother. She crooked her finger, and when Lou went over, she sneaked her a sip from her mug. Lou gasped at the fire in her throat.

"You get used to it," Norma whispered.

"We'll never make it to curtain call otherwise," their mother whispered.

Their father lay down on a bottom bunk and had a smoke. Every few seconds he checked his watch until it was time for the next event—"l.o. Singsong."

"Alrighty," he said after he'd put out the lights. "What do you want to sing?"

"Um," Lou said. "Um," she said again to hear her thin voice, like a pin of light in the pitch black. All she could think of was the Jiminy Cricket encyclopedia song, which their father wouldn't know.

"It's a long way to Tipperary," their father started singing. "Come on! Everybody! Sandy! Norma!"

"It's a long way to go," their mother sang from the bunk in her high, shaky voice.

Sandy squeezed a hand . . . their mother's—she could tell by the smallness. She was half sitting, half lying across their mother's and Norma's legs. The dark didn't scare her anymore up in the house, but in this dark she felt as if she were falling—the whole bed with the three of them on it swirling down. Also there was suddenly a rotting smell that she thought must be Rapunzel, who was buried under the clothesline tree. Was that where the air vent was? Down here, Sandy couldn't tell directions. The smell was so strong, though, that she figured the air vent must be right next to where Rapunzel was.

They sang "The British Grenadiers," "The Battle Hymn of the Republic," "Marching to Pretoria" and "You're a Sap, Mister Jap." Then they switched to songs from Judy Garland movies, singing these quietly. Dulcet tones was what their father demanded for Judy Garland songs, even for "Ballin' the Jack" and "The Trolley Bus Song." They ended with "Somewhere Over the Rainbow." Their father had a really good voice (it sounded even better in the dark, not seeing him singing), and at the last line of "Somewhere Over the Rainbow," the line that goes "Why, oh, why can't I?" where the girls and their mother knew to slow right down, his voice rose clear and smooth as a boy's before their higher voices, making a sound in the blackness so beautiful that they were quiet for a moment afterward.

"We're like stars," Norma said. She meant the stars in the sky.

"Look out, Broadway," their father said. He struck a match, lit a candle and checked his watch. "Twelve on the dot," he said. "Lunch time."

While Lou mixed up the powdered milk and spread margarine on slices of bread, he heated up two cans of spaghetti on the camping stove. They ate sitting on the edge of the bottom bunks. After one mouthful Norma found she wasn't hungry. She gave her plate back to their father and asked if she could go to the toilet.

Her rag was soaking. She couldn't understand how so much blood could be coming out of her and she was still alive. Her stomach didn't hurt any longer, but she was dizzy. What if she really was bleeding to death?

She unpinned the old rag, wrapped it in toilet paper and pinned on another from the pile. On the way back to their mother's bunk she opened the lid of the garbage pail and dropped the balled-up rag in. The pail was lined with polyethylene, and there was a container of disinfectant on the floor for sprinkling inside. She wondered if she bled to death whether he would keep her down here for two weeks.

The Regime said lunch and cleanup were to take one hour, but the dishes were dried and back on the shelves by twelve-forty-two.

"What'll we do until one?" Lou asked, sneaking a sip of their mother's whiskey. One o'clock to three o'clock was cards and board games.

Their father tapped his watch. "I guess we can start the games early," he said grimly. "But tomorrow we stretch lunch out. Eat slower. Talk. I want you all to think up topics of conversation."

He spread a blanket on the floor over the hopscotch, and they sat in a circle. Although their mother never played games in the house, she came over, too, saying that she just couldn't get used to no TV. It was like losing one of your senses, she said, like not being able to see or hear.

Their father reached across the floor for the whiskey and topped up her mug.

First they played cards. Rummy. Usually the girls hated playing cards with him. He told them to hurry up and discard, and then said "Are you kidding?" when they did. He yelled at them to hold their cards up—they were showing everyone their hands. When they won, he said it was luck, but when he won, he said it was eighty percent skill, twenty percent luck. "It's only a game," he told them if they got upset or excited, but he shouted "Yes Momma!" and "Jesus H. Christ!" How the games usually ended was with him either sending them to bed or storming out of the room.

Today, though, because their mother was playing or maybe because he couldn't storm out, he was nicer. He used his nice voice. It made the girls giggle. Everything he said and did, just picking up a card and frowning at it, struck them as really funny.

Over the perfect fan of her cards their mother smiled. She kept winning, a surprise to the girls but not to her, and they realized that rummy must be something else, like sewing and tap dancing, that she was secretly good at.

"Mommy!" they cried, hugging her when she lay down her cards in neat rows, catching them all with mitts-full.

"Well, well," their father said, his smile stopping at the edges of his mouth. The girls laughed. "Settle down," he said nicely.

They were having a great time. It was fun down here; it was like being in a fort. They played hearts next, and their mother went on winning, going for all the cards twice and getting them.

Between deals their father started pacing. "There's something going on," he said, wagging his cigarette at them. "This is a trick on your old dad."

He wanted to play Scrabble, a game of every man for himself. Except that only four could play, so Sandy and their mother were a team.

He went first and made the word *bounce*. That broke the three of them up. Their mother and Sandy make *tinkle,* which was even funnier. Norma used the *b* to make *bust*. They shrieked with laughter. Lou did *fuse,* and they couldn't stand it, it seemed so funny.

"Settle down," their father said again. The vein that was like a fork of lightning down his forehead emerged—a danger sign—but they couldn't stop laughing.

It was his turn. Using the *k*, he made *kidny*.

"Alrighty," he said enthusiastically, starting to add up his score. "Double word—"

"What is it?" Lou asked.

"Kidney," he said. "An organ. Also a bean."

"But kidney's got an *e!*" she cried.

He scowled at the board. "No, it doesn't."

"Well, it does," their mother said. "K-i-d-n-*e*-y."

He laughed. "That's the British spelling. I'm using the American."

Their mother shook her head. "I think there's only the one way to spell it, Jim."

"Daddy, you can't spell," Sandy said tenderly. She couldn't spell either.

"Hey!" Lou cried, rearranging his letters. "You can make *dinky!*"

"Dinky!" Norma cried. They all three burst out laughing.

He hit Lou with a backhand across the face. She fell sideways. Norma and Sandy jumped up and ran to the wall, Sandy crying. Their mother leaned over to grab the whiskey bottle. He stood wearily, as if it was all over, but then he kicked the Scrabble board. It went shooting straight up, scattering letters, bent at the crease down the middle as if it would fly, and fell back to the floor, flat.

Lou, on her feet now, was making leaps at the roof, trying to grab the stairs, which you pulled down.

"The hatch is locked," their father said matter-of-factly. He looked at his watch. "Nap time," he said and began putting out the lights.

Lou threw herself back on the floor. "I'm never going to get up," she said in a passionate voice that persuaded her sisters. Their father stepped over her.

The others went to the bunks. There were two bunks, Lou's and Norma's, on the end wall; one, Sandy's, along the same wall as the toilet; and two more, their mother's and father's, on the wall across from the toilet. Their father climbed up to his bunk carrying a candle, which he held between his knees while he set the alarm clock, then blew it out.

Black. And then that stench. This time all three girls smelled it. Lou imagined it was coming from under the shelter, beneath where she was lying. She started to shiver. The floor was cold and hard and bumpy with Scrabble letters. Her ear throbbed; it seemed huge, a Mouseketeer ear. In Disneyland, with her three bucks, she would have bought Mouseketeer ears.

She got up on her knees and crawled over to where her bunk was, knowing the direction from their father's snores. When she bumped into the bottom bunk, she dropped her head on the edge. She was too tired to climb to the top or even to climb in with Norma.

"Hey," Norma whispered, but Lou was sound asleep. Norma lay her hand on her sister's face. She thought she felt the hot imprint of their father's hand. If she got up now to change her rag, he'd probably hit her, too, but he'd kill her if she leaked all over the bed. She had meant to put on a new rag after the games. "Please, God," she prayed, imploring her flow to stop. Would boys smell the blood? Boys stared at her chest. No matter how smart or nice they were otherwise, they looked stupid and shifty when they stared at her chest. Even on hot days she wore two undershirts and a sweater. She slept on her stomach, but her breasts kept on growing anyway. When would they stop? Sometimes she thought of her breasts as intelligent life with insane, disgusting ambitions.

She wondered if the awful rotting smell was her period.

For some reason the alarm went off at ten after four instead of four o'clock, cutting into their exercise hour. He gave them only a minute each to use the toilet, Norma two minutes to change her rag. The blood hadn't leaked onto her sheets, but it had gone through to her underpants and made a spot on her blue corduroy pants. She would have to wear them like that all week. There was no laundry detergent down here, let alone extra water or time in The Regime for doing a wash, and they had only been allowed to bring down one change of clothing, which they weren't supposed to put on until next Saturday.

Sandy begged for a drink of water, and he let her have a sip. When he was peeing, Lou drank a whole glass. She said she had a headache, and Sandy said, "Same here."

"Have another sip," their mother whispered, tendering her mug.

Afternoon exercises in the dark were next. By admitting that her stomach still hurt, Norma was exempted. Lou and Sandy weren't, pressure headaches being natural down here, their father maintained. No big deal—with the lights out, Lou didn't have any intention of straining herself. She let Sandy hold her hand ("Or I feel like I'm in the Wizard of Oz house," Sandy whispered), and the two of them only pretended to lift their knees as they marched. During touching toes and push-ups they just lay there making grunting noises, while their father's sweat rained on them.

The lights came back on for "Pep Talk." This turned out to be their father telling them about marching for three days on a broken ankle, living for weeks on cans of peaches and dragging a wounded buddy to safety under a barrage of Jerry fire—stories they'd heard a thousand times. Then there was "Inventory," "Supper and Cleanup," then two hours of "Free Time," which was either playing games quietly or reading. The girls played hearts with their mother and sipped from her mug. Lou also sneaked puffs of her cigarette. After a few rounds Norma conked out on the floor. Their father lay on his bunk, smoking and reading his *Life* magazines. Anything about the Russians or about Negroes he read out loud in a sarcastic voice.

At nine o'clock Norma had to wake up, and they all changed into their pajamas. When they were in bed, their father said the soldier's prayer: "Keep our hearts stout and our enemies baffled." He listed their names for God's blessing in the same strange order that they were supposed to use the toilet in. Then he blew out the candle and instantly started to snore. Sandy started to whimper.

"What is it, honey?" their mother asked.

"I smell worms eating Rapunzel."

"That's Daddy."

"I don't think it's a person smell," Norma said quickly, still unsure that it wasn't her.

"It only happens in the dark," Sandy said.

Their mother got up and lit the lantern in the corner by the toilet. "There," she said. "It's gone." And it was. They all went to sleep. An hour or so later, when the alarm rang for their father to crank the blower, he wanted to know who the hell had lit the lantern. "I did, Jim," their mother said. "I've had that nightmare." He turned around and looked at her. What nightmare? the girls wondered. He went back to bed, leaving the lantern burning. Every few hours the alarm went off for him to crank the blower. One of the times, the lantern was out, and he poured in more fuel and lit it again.

. . .

Years later the girls would refer to those two weeks not as "when we were in the fallout shelter" but as "when we almost died."

The threat of death was there from the start, given how hell-bent their father was on keeping them all down there no matter what. As adults the girls agreed that if one of them had a burst appendix, he would have tried to treat her himself with his hunting knife and Bactine.

But since nothing that drastic happened, and since they spent the whole two weeks drunk, how imperilled they were didn't dawn on them until the last days, when there was no more water and when "Pep Talk" was stories of children such as Ann Frank and Little Eva, who faced death bravely.

He marked off the days, scratching lines on the bottom corner of The Regime. By day four the girls and their mother were so attuned to the schedule that they could divine when it was time for the next event. In the middle of games, songs, in the middle of sentences, they would be startled by the thought of what time it was.

Like their mother, the girls could hold their liquor, to the extent, anyway, that they could do what they had to do, but in the mornings they had hangovers, and Norma was usually sick to her stomach as well. At first Norma blamed her period, because she didn't know that you could get drunk on intermittent sips and because she didn't think that their parents would allow them to get drunk. Also because *he* blamed her period. How could he have missed those sips, which were hardly furtive by the second day? Maybe, the three girls thought later (in fact, they thought it was likely), he didn't miss them; likely he saw advantages in keeping them half sedated.

Day four was the best day. His pep talk that day was telling them what a smooth-running machine the five of them were, what a crack squad, what troopers.

Day five, getting out of bed, he stepped on Norma's glasses and shattered both lenses. When it became apparent that they couldn't be fixed with Elmer's glue and electrician's tape, he spanked her for leaving them on the floor, then wrote a letter to the Minister of Health about the crooked optician who'd charged him fifteen bucks extra for unbreakable glass.

All this took up half an hour. "Christ Almighty, eight-thirty-three!" he shouted, and he gave them only a minute each in the bathroom.

Norma didn't waste her minute peeing. She quickly unpinned her rag and felt on the shelf above the toilet for a clean one. She felt all around, knocking over a bottle.

"Time's up!" he yelled.

She patted the ground, found the rag she'd just taken off, and squeezed it out in the toilet.

"Time!" he yelled again.

"Okay, okay." Where had she put the pins?

Lou opened the door and shoved by her to use the toilet. "For God's sake," she said. Norma was standing there with her pajama bottoms down, holding the bloody rag.

"Can you see where my pins are?" Norma whispered.

Lou sat on the toilet and scanned the floor. "Here," she said, picking them up.

"I'm out of rags," Norma said quietly, her voice shaking, her fingers shaking as she took the pins.

Usually after their turns on the toilet they washed in the same order and in the same basin of water that he'd used for shaving. This morning, though, he told them to proceed directly to "Getting Dressed," and to save himself a few seconds, he didn't go with his clothes into the bathroom.

The light stayed on for "Getting Dressed," as this category included shaving and washing. With their father right there, the girls had to cover themselves in their blankets and face the wall to change. Norma, who would have covered herself and faced the wall anyway, even though her sisters and mother had stopped bothering, was close to tears that he was undressing in the same room. Nothing he had ever done seemed so lawless.

"Move it!" he shouted at her, and then her tears did fall because she was holding everyone up and couldn't see, and she was bursting from not having gone to the bathroom, and she felt sick to her stomach, and her rag was leaking.

She couldn't eat. On top of everything else he had made the worst smell ever in the toilet, and he had b.o. from not washing or using deodorant. She sat there stirring her Frosted Flakes, trying to work up the courage to ask if he would rip apart another sheet.

But it was Lou who mentioned that the rags were used up.

He looked at Norma. "Are you still bleeding?" he asked, his tone implying that a real trooper would have stopped by now.

"Like a stuck pig," Lou answered.

"So, take some rags out of the garbage and wash them," he said to Norma. "String up clothesline. Waste not, want not."

Norma retrieved every last rag, in case she went on bleeding for the whole two weeks. Crouched in the bathroom, out of the way, she washed them with dish detergent in the big pot. She couldn't get all the blood out—brownish-red streaked the green cloth. When she tied rope between the upper bunks and hung the rags to dry, their mother said, "Don't they look festive!"

"They look like gas-station flags," Lou said.

What they looked like to Norma were her filth and shame. She would never get over the shame.

How the rest of the day deteriorated:

Their father lost at crazy eights, accused Lou of cheating (she had), spanked her and burned the deck of cards on the stove.

After "Nap Time" Sandy noticed that she was covered in a rash. Their mother diagnosed it as chicken pox.

While perusing the "Pioneers of Self-Defence" pamphlet, their father discovered that when he had been calculating how much water they would need, he had referred to the "For Three Persons" column instead of the "For Five Persons." The dishwater had to last three days. They could only wash and brush their teeth on the even days: eight, ten, and so on. There would be no beverage with lunch.

On the same morning that their father announced these new water-rationing rules, the temperature in the shelter shot up about ten degrees. Their father decided that there must be a heat wave outside and declared it a stroke of luck, a closer temperature to what they could expect from nuclear incineration. He stripped to his boxer shorts and began speaking in his Mexican accent.

After a few hours their mother also stripped, down to her slip, bra and underpants, and she took off Sandy's slacks and sweater. Lou undressed then, too. But Norma, with breasts and bloodstained underpants to hide, kept all her clothes on. To cool herself down she leaned against the concrete walls and wet one of her clean rags with some Canadian Club and wiped her skin. That was what their mother was doing for Sandy's chicken pox, bathing it with a whiskey-soaked dishcloth.

Their mother was as worried and as ferocious as the girls had ever seen her. Defying their father's order to keep Sandy quarantined behind a polyethylene curtain, she let Sandy lie with her. She took her temperature every hour and held the mug of whiskey to her lips. Over and over Sandy pulled the string on her beatnik doll, which was stuck saying, "Hey, cool cat, let's jive." Sandy didn't like a doll to have straight black hair. The only reason she brought this doll down was that their father said she could, and she thought that meant she had to. She pulled the string so that she wouldn't scratch her chicken pox. Their mother kept saying, "I know you feel just terrible," but Sandy didn't, really, other than that she was itchy. Maybe her fever was fooling her, though. Maybe she was dying. Whenever she thought this, she cried.

One of the times that she cried, their mother said, "This child's temperature only has to rise one more degree, and I am taking her out of here, Jim, even if I have to shoot you for the key to the hatch."

"Please God," Lou thought, "let Sandy's temperature go up one degree."

But their mother kept it down with the Canadian Club baths. At least the whiskey cut the toilet smell. The toilet smell was the worst part. That and thirst. From day six (they couldn't understand this, because they were sipping whiskey all day) the girls were parched.

One morning, on day nine, Norma took a drink of the two-day-old dishwater. Poison, probably, but that was fine with her. She was dying anyway. Bleeding to death, and nobody cared. *She* didn't care. To prepare herself for heaven, she had enumerated her sins and asked God's forgiveness. She had conceived a love for Jesus so profound that often during the day she hallucinated harp music and saw the Star of Bethlehem blazing clear. She got the idea that their dead brother sat on the right hand of Jesus, and she carried on long, one-sided conversations with him. From where he sat, he could see the whole world, she imagined. He could even see underground. If they had gone to Disneyland, he'd have watched the tiny dot of their trailer moving across the prairies. Not getting to go to Frontierland is what Norma regretted most. Not seeing the horses. She liked to think that there were horses in heaven—the colored kind with wings. Well, she'd find out soon enough. Every hour that passed and she wasn't dead yet seemed miraculous but illegal. Here she was, eating nothing and losing gallons of blood. A nine-day period so far! Why wasn't she withering away?

The one withering away was Lou, or so Lou thought. Her arms and legs scandalized her. "Look! Look!" she said, holding her arms out. "Sticks!"

There was no argument.

"I need more food!" she cried. "I'm starving!"

"*Tauro guano,*" their father said. "Bullshit."

And because it was true that Lou was eating as much as she ever had, she began to suspect that what was really causing her to lose weight was his bad breath. He was breathing out some kind of DDT gas.

Using one of Norma's washed rags and some string, she made a mask to cover her mouth and nose. In her underwear and the mask, with her hair hanging loose and uncombed, she looked like a night-mare nurse, their father said.

He laughed snidely. He didn't trust her an inch. He wore the can opener tied to the waistband of his boxer shorts in case she tried to sneak food while he was sleeping, and he moved the two remaining jugs of water up to the foot of his bunk.

He called her "the gringo." "Look at the gringo," he said, as though she were out of earshot. "Look at her conniving. If the gringo had her way, she'd undermine the whole exercise."

She already had. Staying down there for fourteen and a half days, for the three hundred and forty-eight hours that the pamphlet recom-mended, was the test, the goal, all that finally counted. It wasn't going to happen. On the morning of the ninth day, before he woke up, Lou added a line to the bottom corner of The Regime where he marked off the days, and he didn't notice.

"Day ten," he announced on his way to the toilet, scratching a horizontal line through the four vertical ones.

That walk to the toilet, including the pause to mark off the day, took six seconds. The day before, he had clocked every one of his functions, noting how long it took to pee, drink a glass of orange juice, play Parcheesi, sing "Easter Parade"—whatever he did. He switched to military time. "Oh eight-hundred," he said. Time obsessed him. There were no more deviations from The Regime, no more lengthening or shortening of events. Even though a lot of the events didn't really happen. "Exercises" had dwindled into Lou and Norma standing on the hopscotch squares, Lou reading comics, Norma staring at blur. The getting dressed part of "Getting Dressed" had stopped altogether, as none of them could be bothered changing into their pajamas at night. He couldn't be bothered washing, brushing his teeth and shaving, either, by day ten. He looked like a hobo, like the men who wandered out of the ravine to pull down their pants in public. From thirst he had started in on the whiskey.

Alcohol made him clumsy and made him cry. During nap time on day eleven, which was really day ten, Lou tried to mark off another day on The Regime, but this time he caught her, and when he spanked her, he and Sandy were the ones who burst into tears.

On day twelve he dropped the last jug, and all the water spilled onto the floor.

"You idiot!" Lou screamed, but he was too stunned to respond. Yanking off her mask, Lou fell to her knees and lapped at the water. That was it for unadulterated fluid. For the next sixty-one hours it was whiskey or nothing.

Those hours were a sweet, sewery dream. It helped that their father was plastered. He still made an attempt to announce some of The Regime events on the button, but whether or not the events happened, he didn't notice.

"A cheap drunk," Lou said as he lay passed out on the floor during

"Inventory" and she was unclipping the can opener from his boxer shorts.

Now they could eat what they liked when they liked. But they weren't that hungry. Cans with juice in them—the vegetable and fruit cans—were the only ones that interested them, although for some reason they weren't that thirsty anymore either.

Why didn't Lou search for the key to the hatch one of those times when he was dead to the world? She asked herself this the day after they were out of the shelter, and she wondered about it for the rest of her life. Why didn't she escape? She was drunk, there was that, but no more so than when she marked off a day on The Regime. As a matter of fact, she was clear-headed enough to realize that she *was* drunk and that she wasn't a cheap drunk.

Their mother took over "Singsong" and "Pep Talk." Instead of singing soldier songs, they sang television-show theme songs and songs from old musicals. Instead of hearing stories about the war and the Great Depression, they heard old TV-show episodes and stories about their mother growing up on a farm, an only daughter who worshipped the ground her two older brothers walked on, who always wore white and was the model for the Dutch Cleanser girl.

Even after her fever was gone, Sandy continued to sleep with their mother. The two of them spent most of the day in bed, napping or gazing at the ceiling (Sandy had picked up their mother's serene gaze). Looking at them lying there, golden and the same, Lou could imagine they were either corpses or angels. Sometimes Lou thought they were from outer space, spying Martians in human form who figured that to do a daughter disguise, you just made a smaller mother.

Lou spent her free time practicing how to deal from the bottom of the deck, reading the *Life* magazines now that their father wasn't, and working on her lists, alphabetizing and adding to her list of swear words and extending her hit list to include famous people, such as the Avon lady and Kathy from "Father Knows Best."

Norma drank from her own whiskey bottle, which she held to her chest like a cross, a ticket to heaven. Without her glasses on she felt as if she were in heaven already, as if she were in a cloud surrounded by the dear, featureless faces of her family. Never had she known such tranquility. She was tranquil every minute of those final hours except once—when she went to the bathroom to change her rag, and their father was already there, standing in front of the toilet.

"Oh, are you going to use it?" she asked, supposing that he wasn't, because he'd left the door open and hadn't told her to go away.

And then she realized, from the blur of skin color, that his pants were already down.

She turned, stumbled out the door. "I can't see," she cried.

But she *had* seen. She'd seen his penis, the purply, fuzzy shape of it, sticking out.

She thought, panicking, "He knows I saw." She took a sip of whiskey. "He's just drunk," she told herself. "He doesn't know what he's doing." She stared at the glow of the lantern, its everlasting, godly glow, and remembered a hymn: "Above the clear, blue sky, in heaven's bright abode." She could hardly wait.

At five o'clock on the morning of the final day their father emptied the remaining three whiskey bottles onto the floor.

"We're leaving here sober, goddamnit," he said.

Their mother excluded, of course. Before emptying the bottles, he filled her mug, but she wouldn't share.

The previous night they'd eaten a can of tomatoes, the last can of food that contained liquid, leaving only five-day-old dishwater to drink. It seemed better than nothing.

By noon all three girls had the worst headaches they'd ever had in their lives. There were still six hours to go.

"I'm dying," Lou said. "Now I really am dying."

Sandy cried. Norma felt like crying, too. She was aware again of how the place smelled, how *she* smelled. She was tormented by having presumed that someone as smelly and blind and hungover as she was could go to heaven.

All that the three of them wanted to do was sleep, but their father made them fold the bedding and reassemble and pack the boxes. He chain-smoked. Checked his watch every two minutes. He kept threatening to give Lou a fat lip if she didn't shut up. His hands shook. Stuck to his face were bits of toilet paper from where he'd cut himself shaving. He looked a wreck. They all did.

At five o'clock he had them sit on the edges of their bunks holding what they would carry up. They fixed their eyes on the hatch as though it would open by itself, as though, if it didn't, they were trapped forever.

The sun was blinding. The house was still there. The grass was there under their feet, in need of a cut. A neighbor's dog barked. Between their house and the house next door a blue car skimmed past. They all gaped at it. They stood close together, squinting.

"Home sweet home," their father said, which is what he said after a long car ride or a holiday. His eyes were triumphant, crazy, miserable.

WHITE OVERNIGHT

1963

Their father begins sleeping in the living room, stashing his blankets, pillow and pajamas behind the chesterfield each morning. Their mother looks stupefied at breakfast. In September she goes into the hospital. The girls come home to find their father sitting at the kitchen table, stabbing a cigarette butt into a salad bowl heaped with butts.

"Your mother's having her appendix out," he says.

"She's already had it out," Lou says. They saw the scar when she had the flu, that time when they had to take her to the toilet.

He glances at them, goes on stabbing the butt. "No, she hasn't," he mutters. "That was something else."

"What?"

"An operation. A complication." He looks straight at Lou. "When *you* were born, as a matter of fact."

Their mother is gone for two weeks. In the evenings their father drives to see her with a bottle of whiskey in his briefcase. When she returns home, her hair is white. She has gone white overnight.

A reaction to the anesthetic, their father explains. But the sag of her small shoulders, the grey around her eyes, the whole deleted look of her says she's suffered more than that. The girls don't ask. They don't want to know. Sandy can't look at her without thinking of the white-haired Santa Claus man who died on them. She can't comb her own gold hair without worrying about being their mother's image and turning into an old lady at thirty-six.

Several weeks later Aunt Betty delivers Mary Jane's last winter's wardrobe for their mother to refashion into wardrobes for them. Every day after school the girls open the front door expecting to hear the sewing machine. Instead they see the unopened boxes, still there in the hall. Eventually Norma selects what she wants (she is the only one who can wear the clothes unaltered), and their father stores the rest under the stairs.

Sandy cries to see the boxes go. Down in the basement she takes the party dresses and blouses and jumpers out and strokes the expensive material.

Then one day, one Saturday morning, she goes down with scissors and the portable sewing machine. By dinner she has a skirt—a tight blue wool with yellow buttons up one side, made from a jumper. By Sunday afternoon she has a matching vest. She wears the outfit to school on Monday, and everyone thinks it came from a store.

For the rest of the week and all the next week, after school, before school, she sews. At lunchtime she draws patterns and runs over in her mind what piece of clothing she'll rip apart and work with next. The whole time she has a feeling of learning a skill already mastered. She makes a puff-sleeved, scallop-collared blouse out of a dress, a pleated skirt out of a full one, a dress out of a dress. She unravels and reknits a sweater.

Only Norma appreciates that for Sandy to be making the kinds of clothes she is without being shown how, and at her age, is amazing. Although she doesn't praise Sandy (she has a feeling these days that nothing her sisters do is any of her business), she does keep her in material by returning most of the clothes she took out of the boxes. It occurs to her that she should write up a will and bequeath Sandy her wardrobe—all except for the outfit that she'll be buried in.

Norma devotes a lot of thought to what this outfit will be. Lately she finds herself worrying about her funeral, as if it's a school project she hardly has any time to complete. Something she keeps meaning to find out is whether the mortician puts your glasses on you. She worries about enough people showing up. She wonders if even their mother will. Lou will have to—their father will force Lou to go—but will Lou cry? It bothers Norma that she can't picture Lou crying. Lou almost never cries, but why Norma can't picture it, and would like to, is that all of a sudden Lou seems to hate her. Porko, Lou calls her, or Lard Ass—nothing else. For no reason at all she'll say, "This is what's wrong with you. Mud-brown hair, pudgy red cheeks, Coke-bottle glasses, basketball tits, big fat ass."

Norma doesn't defend herself. How can she, when it's all true? And she doesn't strike back with a list of what's wrong with the way Lou looks, because she can only think of one thing and because she's afraid that if she starts being cruel, she won't be able to stop—she'll go all the way to murderer—and because, with their brother being dead, it's up to her to be the strong one.

And because she can take it. Nothing Lou could ever say could be as bad as school, and if Norma can take school, she can take anything. She's in her first year of high school. All of her old friends are in another class. She eats lunch with an adenoidal girl who calls her Norba and who is always saying "Who cares?"

But it beats eating alone. When Norma walks down the corridors alone, boys moo at her and call her Enorma. A rumor is going around that she has three breasts. In the gym change-room she catches girls trying to get a look. Finally she starts changing in one of the toilet cubicles, going through the whole act of tearing off a piece of toilet paper and flushing.

She lives for three-fifteen, when she can go home and down to their father's workroom. There, except for the companionable hum of the sewing machine in the next room, there is quietness. If she doesn't have laundry to do, she has a full two hours to herself.

The sight of the tools hanging above the workbench in their logical rows always stirs her. She wishes she could build a whole room again, she and their father. She thinks of when they built the fallout shelter together as when she was young and carefree. Then she worked with eight-foot-long two-by-fours. Now she works with pieces from the scrap pile. This is one of their father's conditions, the other being that whatever she makes has to serve a useful function.

The first thing she makes is a knick-knack holder. She is finished and looking for a place to hang it before she realizes that they don't have knick-knacks (or needlepoint pictures, or plastic fishes on the wall). She ends up hanging it beside her bed to put her glasses and drink of water on at night.

Next she makes a bread box. Then a jewelry box, then a toolbox. She knows that she isn't as skilful at carpentry as Sandy is at sewing, but she comes up with good ideas, such as adding hooks to the toolbox so that it can hang on a ladder. In their father's workroom her brain flowers with so many ideas that she stops dwelling on her funeral.

One day she discovers an accordion file under the workbench. It's all dusty and tied up with a long black shoelace. She is reminded of the newspaper cutting that Uncle Eugene hid in his workroom. As she opens the file and takes out what's inside—a black-and-white photograph—that cutting about their brother, Jimmy, is at the front of her mind, and yet she thinks the photograph is her. In one of the albums there's a picture of her at six months, and she looks exactly like this: black hair, eyes at a Chinese slant, even wearing the same lace nightgown.

Why is their father hiding the picture down here? she wonders. Her little baby hands are palms up in a "Who, me?" gesture. Did he get a kick out of that? Maybe he really loved her when she was a baby.

She turns the picture over. "Jimmy," she reads out loud, "March second, nineteen forty-eight."

She turns the picture back round. "Jimmy Field," she says softly, formally.

He could have been her identical twin. When she was born, their mother and father must have wondered if she was him, back from the bottom of Niagara Falls. She looks at the writing. Small, tidy letters. Their mother's.

"Poor baby, poor little baby," she says to the face. Now that she knows it's Jimmy's, she thinks it's darling. "Mommy loved you. Did she ever. When you drowned, she turned to drink."

She kisses the picture, slips it back in the file, ties up the shoelace and puts the file where she found it under the bench. For the rest of that afternoon she is aware of the picture at thigh level, like a beam of warm light hitting her, a comfort.

About a week later she's standing there at the workbench, and she finds herself saying out loud: "What would you do if you were a girl, and boys mooed at you?" She imagines the answer formulating in Jimmy's head, beaming out to her thighs and then travelling up through her body to her brain. She imagines a voice like Jesus's: "Pretend you are Daniel in the lion's den."

From that day on she asks Jimmy all of her pressing questions. She spaces them out and restricts them to important issues, feeling that she should show respect. To every question that she asks, she receives an answer that she knows is right. "Why not see what needs repairing around the house?" "Our father is in a great mood these days—ask if you can use some of his good pieces of wood."

Suddenly their father is a pal, a big spender. He arrives home with gifts of chocolate bars. He increases their allowance. One Saturday in October he shows up from work at noon, raving about the gorgeous fall colors, and makes them drive with him to the country to see the trees. They haven't gone on a drive to the country in years, not since their mother stopped leaving the house. For about two hours, without him once complaining about what the pot holes are doing to his shocks, they drive up and down rough roads. He smiles ecstatically, whistles, starts up singsongs. Then he drives back into the city, right downtown, though he says it means skipping an important meeting at work. Every ethnic neighborhood they enter he announces, letting go of the steering wheel for a second and shouting through cupped hands. "Now entering Wopville!" "Now entering Humpadonia!" The girls are glad the car windows are shut. On the way home he stops at a restaurant and buys them deluxe sundaes. "What the hell," he laughs when he sees the bill.

Where's his bad temper? Lou can even swear in front of him, and if he doesn't ignore her, all he says is something like, "What a character," or "You slay me."

At first Lou thinks, "This is great," but after about a week he gets on her nerves.

Like everybody else these days. These days everybody makes her want to throw up. With one exception—Sherry, her new friend. Sherry is from Chicago. She moved up to live with an aunt because her mother had a nervous breakdown after her father fell in love with "a piece of black tail." Lou is the only girl in her class who knows that this isn't an animal.

Sherry can't get over how innocent the girls up north are. "No girl in Chicago would be caught dead without makeup," she says. Whenever Lou calls on her, no matter what time it is, she has on orange pancake, pink lipstick and black eyeliner. At school she always wears a tight cardigan sweater buttoned up backwards. She and Lou smoke cigarettes behind the school and talk to each other in Southern accents like Sandra Dee's in *Tammy Tell Me True*. "I'm feeling all funny peculiar," they say. "I'm feeling all cotched in a tree." When a high-school boy comes along and wants Sherry to neck with him, Lou keeps a lookout. "I'm feeling all pleasured for sure," Sherry says afterward.

Despite appearances, Lou knows that between the two of them she's the bad influence. Sherry necks with boys, smokes the cigarettes Lou steals and dresses like a sex maniac. That's it. Underneath she's as nice as a Sunday-school teacher. "She's not so bad," she'll say, or "She can't help it," when Lou gets carried away lambasting somebody. She always looks on the bright side. "Beats living with a mental mother," is what she says about having to leave Chicago. Anyway, she says, in a few years she's going to start marrying old, rich men, having sex with them until they die of heart attacks and then spending all their loot.

"Why don't you marry rich, *young* men and murder them?" Lou suggests. Sherry tells her she has a big mean streak.

Lou has an even bigger angry streak. Sometimes she gets so angry that she goes out after dark and throws stones at windows and streetlights. One night she writes, "FUCK OFF" in white chalk all down the road and on people's fences.

In her dreams she is another person, gentle and innocent, often still a little girl. She has a recurring dream in which she and her sisters live peacefully by themselves in the white mansion where the old man died on them.

In real life she hates living with her sisters, especially with Norma. Norma drives her crazy—eating like a pig, fat as a pig, letting boys get away with calling her names. Lou can't stand anyone being mean to Norma. She throws a full bottle of Coke at a boy who moos at Norma when she and Norma are coming out of the smoke shop. Whenever she sees Norma from far away, at the end of the street, for instance, walking home from school (always alone), her throat tightens. She wants Norma never to hurt again. She wants to save Norma's life! Instead, she yells at her. She can't help it. Every time she turns around, it seems, Norma is stuffing herself with cookies. Or doing one of Lou's jobs. Washing the dishes. Making the lunches. "What are you trying to prove!" Lou rages, tears welling in her eyes.

One day, she's had enough. She says, "Okay, you want to do everything around here, go ahead. I quit."

The only chore Lou will still do is the grocery shopping, because that's when she picks up her weekly supply of pop and candy. Saturday mornings their father drives her and her wagon to the store on his way to work—"The early bird catches the worm," he says (you can stake your life on it)—but she usually goes straight from the car to Sherry's place in the apartment buildings behind the shopping center and doesn't get around to buying the groceries until the afternoon.

One Saturday she leaves it a bit late and flies through the supermarket doors just as the manager is about to lock up. "Five minutes," he warns.

"See ya in three," Lou says, dropping her wagon handle and grabbing a cart. Since she buys the same things every week, she moves fast.

She seems to be the last customer in the store. It increases her speed. But as she's racing to the meat counter, she sees two people standing in front of the hotdog section, right in front of where she's headed. One is a woman in a clerk's coat, and one is a man in a black topcoat.

A strange woman.

And their father.

Lou comes to a stop, her running shoes squealing. Their father doesn't turn around. The woman, who is standing too near to their father, facing him and Lou, glances over. Her name is written on her breast pocket. Lou reads it, she's that close. "Vera Produce," she reads.

She says, "Dad." But the word seems to slam into a brick wall just outside her mouth. Their father is gripping Vera Produce's left hand, holding it low and tight against her red skirt.

Against her hip. She has wide hips and big white legs with no nylons. Red high heels. She glances at Lou again, glances at someone else who is walking up the next aisle.

"The store is closing," a voice says over the P.A. "Please take your purchases to the checkout. The store is closing." Vera Produce combs her fingers through her black hair. Their father whispers something to her. She shakes her head at the ground, looking crabby, then looks back up at him with a sprawling, wet face.

"Honey," their father says. He lays his hand on the side of her head. She drops her red lips to the cuff of his shirt that yesterday Norma scorched with the iron and soaked in straight bleach. Tears pouring out of her eyes, Vera Produce kisses a line from their father's cuff to the tips of his fingers.

Lou lets go of her shopping cart. She turns, leaving the cart and her groceries, and marches back down the aisle to the front of the store. The manager has to unlock the door for her. "Don't forget your wagon," he says.

The minute she steps outside, the parking-lot lights come on. In the farthest row, by the Salvation Army bin, she spots their father's station wagon. Hiding there, like dirty underpants thrown behind a door. She won't go past it. She goes the other way, the long way home. She is familiar with the calm she is feeling; she recognizes it as temporary. She walks slowly, pulling her empty wagon, starting and stopping, looking into windows that she has no inclination to break. Everyone is having supper around kitchen tables. In front of one house, which is exactly like theirs—it even has a spindly willow tree in the middle of the lawn, and the same front door with three round windows going up at a slant like how you know a character in a comic book is thinking—she sits down in her wagon. Then she lies down, testing out what kind of bed it'll make.

His car isn't in the garage. Lou has a quick, repellent image of him and Vera necking in the parking lot. Vera Produce has fat white legs like the pillars in front of a mansion. What does their father see in her? What does she see in him?—that's the real question. Vera Produce must be crazy. A crazy piece of tail.

Lou pulls the wagon into the middle of the garage for him to crash into, then kicks it over to the wall out of the way. It makes her sick to think how he's been playing them all for suckers with his nice-guy act. Who will pay the bills if he runs off? After Sherry's father ran off with the Negro woman, Sherry's mother was forced to sell the house.

Inside, the TV is blaring. Norma is hammering.

"Why can't we ever have any goddamn peace and quiet around here!" Lou screams.

Instantly there is silence. A moment later Norma comes up from the basement and into the front hall. She's wearing a pair of their father's old work pants with the cuffs rolled up and one of their cousin Mary Jane's gigantic cardigans, flaked with sawdust. "Where are the groceries?" she asks.

Lou takes her jacket off. Instead of dropping it on the bench, she hangs it on a hanger in the closet.

"What's going on?" Norma says.

Lou shoves by her into the kitchen. She wonders whether or not to tell the truth. Norma follows her, asking about the groceries again. Sighing, Lou drops onto a chair. She looks at Norma's anxious face and notices for the first time that it's their father's, only with glasses and younger and fatter. And nicer. Sandy's face is their mother's. Mine, Lou thinks, is nobody's. It's going to be awful, she thinks, not doing anything that might make him mad, being good all the time so that he'll want to stay here. She folds her arms on the kitchen table and rests her head on her hands. Right now she hasn't the energy or the heart to give Norma the bad news. "I forgot," she says.

"Forgot?"

"Yeah, forgot. Okay?"

More than the obvious lie, more than no groceries and hanging up the jacket, the tone of Lou's voice worries Norma. What has Lou done? Lou was the one who scrawled that filth all over the roads and fences a couple of weeks ago. (Norma wiped off as much as she could with her scarf.) Aside from recognizing the writing—the same *F,* like the twice-crossed *T,* that Lou uses to sign their last name—Norma can't think of anyone else who would go that far. She knows that Lou steals and hangs around with the loose girl from Chicago. "Protect your sisters," their brother, Jimmy, advises from heaven. Easy to say.

"Well," Norma says, sighing, helpless as always, "I guess it's mustard sandwiches for dinner."

. . .

They wait for their father before starting to eat. Every few minutes Lou checks at the window. After a quarter of an hour she says quietly, "The son of a bitch isn't coming back," and Norma wraps his sandwich in wax paper for him to eat later.

His car pulls up just as they're sitting down at the table. "Come on," Lou says, dashing out to the front hall.

Their father seems surprised to see them. "Fine, at ease," he says without inspecting their outstretched hands. He frowns past them at the dining room, as if he's in the wrong house.

"I got sick, so there's no groceries," Lou says. She can't keep the resentment out of her voice. As he's hanging up his coat, she sees Vera's red lipstick on his shirt cuff.

"What?" he says remotely, turning around.

When Lou doesn't answer, Norma murmurs, "Lou was too sick to do the shopping."

"Oh, that's okay," their father says. He pats Lou on the shoulder, then walks down the hall to his and their mother's bedroom, going in and shutting the door without a sound, as they have never known him to shut a door.

MORTIFIED BY DESIRE

1967

Sandy goes out with lots of boys, almost any boy who asks her. A couple of nights ago a boy told her he loved her and pleaded with her to go steady.

"Well, okay," she said at last, seeing as he loved her.

They were sitting in his car in her driveway. They kissed, and she floated a long way away from all of him except for his mouth. She forgot who he was—she thought he was the boy she went out with the week before—and when she opened her eyes, his face gave her a start.

"What's the matter?" he asked.

She said, "I've changed my mind," thinking she'd better.

"Why?"

But she wouldn't tell him, she wouldn't be that mean. He slammed his hand on the steering wheel and called her a tease. He said she had come between him and his best friend, did she know that? She shook her head. She didn't even know who his best friend was. At this point the kitchen light came on, and she jumped out of the car, afraid that their father had been spying from the window.

Their father hates her going out on dates. But when she was thirteen and getting asked out, he said: "When you're sixteen." And when she turned sixteen, and he tried to go back on his word, their mother surprised them both with one of her rare interventions. "Let the child kick up her heels," she said, quoting something, her sad, lost voice evidently striking their father where it counted, because he gave in.

But he still delivers lectures about male hormones running wild. And the home for unwed mothers is never far from his thoughts. (He claims that the girls there have to eat without knives because they're so depressed and ashamed, they're liable to stab themselves.) When he catches Sandy wearing makeup, he demands that she hand over her tubes and eye pencils. If she wears a tight skirt or sweater, or even if she wears high heels, he calls her Hooker and Pickup Artist.

At least he never hits her—Norma and Lou he would have. Lou says that what saves her is looking like their mother. She says, "Tell him to go fuck himself. What have you got to be afraid of?"

That one day he *will* hit her. When he yells at her, she cries in case he's on the brink. And yet she'd rather stab herself like an unwed mother than leave the house dressed out of fashion. As treacherous as it makes her feel toward their mother, she wishes that he'd find another girlfriend and be nice again.

Not that their mother seems to mind about his girlfriends. She talks about them as if they're the cars he borrows from the lot at work. It's their mother, as a matter of fact, who told Sandy about the girlfriends. Sweetie pies, she calls them. One day, after six months of him not losing his temper once, he hit Lou across the face for taking cigarettes from his dresser drawer. Sandy ran crying into the TV room, and their mother said that he must have broken up with his latest sweetie pie.

"We're all going to have to be patient with him," she said, wiping Sandy's tears. "We're all going to have to dance on eggs for a while."

That was a year ago. But last night he brought gifts home—three pairs of knitted duck-head slippers—so Sandy had her fingers crossed because, thinking back, she's figured out that gifts are the first sign.

Only Norma put her slippers on. It struck Lou right away that she could sell hers to a kid she babysits, and Sandy decided to take hers into work, to show the other girls, she told their father, but actually to give them to Mrs. Dart, who has an eight-year-old daughter.

Mrs. Dart is Sandy's boss at the fabric store. Thursday and Friday evenings and all day Saturday Sandy sells fabric on a straight commission basis. Last month she was the top part-time salesgirl in the entire chain, coast to coast, which meant that she won a bolt of fabric of her choice (she picked blue velvet) and got her picture on the front page of the store newsletter.

"You have a model's face," the other salesgirls told her. "Too bad you're not taller."

But Mrs. Dart said that Sandy was destined for greater things. Sandy was going to be a fashion designer, Mrs. Dart said.

Mrs. Dart is always praising Sandy to the skies. The least Sandy can do is to give her the slippers. Although Mrs. Dart is tall, black-haired, wears glasses and too much makeup, uses bad language and has Parkinson's disease, she maintains that Sandy is her, twenty years ago. Everything Sandy wears (Sandy designs and makes all her own clothes), Mrs. Dart raves about. "I used to sew like that," she says, "before I got the shakes." Her theory is that Sandy's clothes are her magic sales formula, that they draw in customers like flies to horse-shit, if Sandy will pardon her French. It seems to be the case. Sandy isn't pushy, but she's the one that most of the women approach.

On the Saturday that Sandy brings in the slippers, not just she but all the salesgirls have a lineup of customers. This is because it's Bargain Bonanza Day. If a customer purchases three yards of any material, she gets two yards of another material of similar value, free. By 10:30 Sandy has racked up sixty dollars' worth of sales.

"It's like a ceremonial war," a man says.

Sandy looks at him, surprised. You don't get many men in here.

He picks up a bolt of paisley. "All you girls running around with your clubs," he says, tapping the bolt on her shoulder. "Barging into each other. But no injuries. No deaths."

"Not yet," she says.

He laughs, a genuinely amused laugh that is suddenly bouncing inside her chest. She's in the middle of cutting three yards of pink silk, and she has to stop halfway and wait for the ball behind her heart to go still.

"Three yards," her customer says impatiently.

When she finishes cutting, she keeps her head lowered as she folds the material. His legs are before her eyes. Rust-brown tweed trousers, expensive-looking. Made in Italy, she'd bet.

He puts the bolt of paisley down and follows her to the front desk. Her fingers on the cash register keys are wet. Even out of the tips of her fingers she's perspiring.

But he's not good-looking, she thinks. As she hands the customer her change, she glances at him. Stocky, balding, old—thirty-five, maybe forty.

He smiles. His eyes are forest green with primrose yellow flecks. Like a sweater she's knitting. "Do they let you out for coffee?" he asks quietly.

She nods.

"When?"

"Oh, any time now."

"Meet me at the doughnut shop," he says. "Five minutes."

She checks the watch hanging on the side of the cash register. "Half an hour," she says.

He's already walking out. He raises his fist, thumb up, to show that half an hour is fine.

"I'll be right with you," she says to the next customer. She goes to the back of the store, into the washroom, shuts the door, sits on the toilet seat and covers her face with hands. Her hands are still wet. She turns them over and studies each perfect Peach Blossom Pink nail with the feeling that she's looking at them for the last time.

After supper and washing the dishes, making lunches for the next day and maybe putting through a load of laundry, Norma has about fifteen minutes left to do what she wants. Usually she's so exhausted, she just lies on the floor in front of the TV. At eight o'clock she has to get up, go to her and Lou's room, and sit at her desk until it's time for bed.

Those two and a half hours of studying every night, Sunday to Friday, are her Regime. Their father summoned that bomb-shelter word back after she failed grade twelve last year. Before then she kept her grades from him by getting their mother to sign her report cards. But when you fail, both parents have to sign, and there are meetings with the vice-principal, and letters back and forth.

On the long walk home last spring, on the final day of school, Norma didn't bother asking God for the miracle that their father wouldn't hit her. She deliberately stepped out into traffic, but all the cars stopped, and a truck driver hung out his window and yelled, "Get outta the road, fat ass." Running back to the curb, she found herself whimpering their dead brother's name.

She will always believe that Jimmy heard her. No matter what else she will later renounce, she will always hold it in her heart that it was because of Jimmy that their father didn't lift a finger.

Their father was between girlfriends, and it took nothing to get him mad, but all he did after looking over her report card that evening was deliver a speech, featuring examples from his life in the army, about the need for a person to stick to a rigid routine of work. "Do you read me?" he asked every few minutes, and she answered, "Yes, yes." Naturally, she didn't ruin a good thing by telling him what she really needs.

Which, most likely, is a psychiatrist. She has a mental illness that she's never heard of. Exam-room phobia, she calls it. The instant she enters the gym, where exams are written, and she sees those lines of desks, vertigo strikes her. Her head spins, and sweat seems to flood out from under her arms and between her breasts, and she feels that if the flood doesn't stop, it will become an avalanche of sweat, and she will be swept down with the torrent.

Once, two years ago, she fainted at the gym doors and was carried by three boys ("It *took* three boys," was how she was informed) to the nurse's office. But she passed the exam. She got honors, in fact, because she was allowed to write it after school, by herself in an empty classroom. That was how she learned that exam rooms, not exams, are what she is terrified of.

Tell the vice-principal, her girlfriends said. Ask permission to write every exam alone.

"I'll get over it," Norma said, and her friends knew that this meant she didn't want to draw attention to herself.

Her friends are in the same boat. One of them is six foot three, one has chronic acne, and one is the adenoidal girl. Like Norma, they wear thick glasses, and that's all the four of them have in common, aside from being considered lepers.

Of the many things Norma regrets about herself, she regrets most not having the guts to drop these girls. She's never disliked anybody who tormented her, yet she can't stand these girls, who are loyal and protective and haven't once hurt her feelings.

Everyone thinks they're as nice as they pretend to be, as nice as girls compensating for their appearance are supposed to be. But the truth is, they're vicious. They hate any girl who doesn't have a socially debilitating defect. All some normal girl has to do is walk by their table in the cafeteria and the three of them are off, nattering to each other about how stupid, loose and, underneath the clothes and makeup, how really homely the girl is. Listening to them, Norma longs for a pretty friend. Pretty girls, like her sister Sandy, stay sweet as babies. Ugly girls are rotten; their outer ugliness rots them inside.

Norma doesn't exempt herself. She isn't hateful, but she feels that what she is inside is worse, in a way—that she is cowardly and secretive and that this is even more despicable than being cruel. She never tells her friends anything important about herself. At giving vague, misleading answers she is masterful. She even keeps where she lives secret, each afternoon parting with her friends at the bottom of her street and then meeting them there the next morning. Once, when the tall girl asked if she could stop by Norma's house to go to the bathroom, Norma just said lamely, "Oh, you can hold it," and walked away. She might have dredged up that old story about their mother being sick, but she has become incapable of the direct lie. Because she is so sneaky and cowardly, she thinks.

She thinks that all the crosses she bears, all the housework, the study regime, the name-calling, the loneliness, are her just deserts.

He's the only customer in the doughnut shop. He's in the last booth, facing the door, smoking a cigarette.

"Well, what do you know about that?" he says, smiling. "She showed up."

"I always take my break here," Sandy says, sliding into the seat across from him.

"Want one?" He extends the pack of Players.

"I don't smoke." She twists around to study the doughnut menu, although she always orders a chocolate glaze. When he offered her a cigarette, she noticed that he was wearing a chain bracelet. She doesn't like jewelry on men. She doesn't like bald spots.

"You're one beautiful doll," he says.

She twists back round.

"Has anyone ever told you you're beautiful?"

She nods. Does he think he's the first? She tried to see what it is about him that made her perspire in the store, but she only sees how old he is.

"What are those big blue eyes staring at?" he says, laughing.

Her face burns. That's what she likes—his laugh.

He orders two coffees and two cherry-filled doughnuts. When the waitress leaves them, he lights another cigarette and says, "Sandra Field. Sweet sixteen. Youngest of three sisters. Popular as hell but no steady boyfriend, though I find that hard to believe."

She feels a rush of familiar dread. "How do you know all that?"

"I asked."

"Who?"

He shakes his head, smiling.

She leans into the table. "*Who?*"

"Can't reveal my sources, now can I?"

She clings to the edge of the seat, touching the ridge of hard chewing gum underneath. Has he found out that their mother dropped their brother over Niagara Falls? No, that's crazy. Who would tell him that? But this is what happens when boys—men—pry into her life. "I want to know everything about you," they say, and what always happens is that her mind plunges straight down to her deepest secret.

"Hey. Doll." He attempts to lift her chin. She doesn't let him. His thumb traces the line of her jaw, and then his hand is gone and picking his cigarette out of the aluminum ashtray.

"Okay," he says. "Fair's fair. Reg Sherman. Thirty-eight years young. Only child. Former Albert Park High School quarterback. Present proprietor of Sherman Shoes."

She looks at him. Sherman Shoes is next to the fabric store, and now she remembers that she's seen him before. He's the man who sold her her blue ankle-strap heels. She remembers that he held her foot for too long and squeezed her toes, but so gently, the way a doctor feels for breaks.

"Part-time spy," he goes on. "Current mission—get the lowdown on one Miss Sandra Field." He laughs, and she does, too, because his laugh makes her delirious.

"Married," he says.

She laughs into her paper napkin.

"Fifteen years," he says, shaking his head, and she realizes he isn't joking.

He grasps her arm. His married man's hand on her arm is plum-colored under the black hair. Why didn't it occur to her that someone his age would be married?

"Look," he says. "I want to be honest with you. I'm married. Unhappily, but there's nothing I can do about it. I've got two kids. Great kids."

She waits.

"It doesn't make any difference," he says.

She doesn't know what he means.

"Sandra. . . ." He lets go of her arm. "God. Look at you. You're a living doll, you know that?"

"I better get back," she says, reading the time upside down on his wristwatch.

"Let's go for a drive," he says enthusiastically.

"Now?"

"Sunday. Sunday afternoon."

So that's what he's after. A girlfriend on the side. A sweetie pie to keep him happy.

"Come on," he says. "You'll get to ride in my new car."

"Oh, okay," she says, partly because her break is over, partly because if he's anything like their father, it's not as though his wife and kids will care.

The insulation and two-by-fours and top-of-the-line knotty pine have been piled downstairs for over a year. Their father bought it all one day during a week of craziness. The next day he decided to send it back but couldn't because the sale was final. That got him so mad that he threw the vacuum cleaner through the wall between the dining room and the front hall, making a boot-shaped hole, which is still there. He gave Lou a shiner that week, ran the car into a streetlight, and one night, thinking he heard a prowler in the backyard, got his World War II gun from the bomb shelter and accidentally shot himself in the foot. Now he's lame.

Norma knows the reason for his crackup and for him being in a terrible mood ever since. Lou told her. Not realizing that their mother and Sandy also knew, they decided to keep it to themselves.

"They couldn't take it," Lou said.

"No," Norma agreed. She wasn't sure that she could take it either. She went down to their father's workroom and made a footstool for their beautiful, prematurely white-haired little mother.

Now, a year later, the fact that their father fools around is just another secret. Norma had hoped he'd stopped, but a couple of weeks ago he brought home three pairs of duckhead slippers. To show him, and to take advantage of his good mood, she starts fixing up the basement. All year she's been dying to get her hands on that wood, and one Saturday she goes downstairs and saws a piece of the knotty pine in half. It feels death-defying, though not brave. Out of control is more like it.

But not reckless, either. She wants to do the job right. She consults the man who owns the hardware store about the wiring and insulation, and she buys a book called *So You Want to Build a Rec Room?* What she can't find out, she figures out. It only takes common sense, and common sense is her big attribute, the one thing about her that people find to praise. In three afternoons she installs fluorescent lighting and two new outlets. Then she begins to strap the walls.

Their father finally notices what's going on. He arrives home early one night, in time for supper (Lovergirl—Lou's name for all his women—must be busy), and after inspection goes to the basement for a beer. "What the heck . . . ," he says at the bottom of the stairs. A month ago, before Lovergirl, he'd have said what the hell. He calls Norma to come down. "Who did all this?" he asks.

"Me," she says sullenly. She knows he won't hit her.

"You? By yourself?"

She nods.

"But how the heck did you know how?" He is looking straight at her.

She won't answer, she won't tell him.

He goes over to the wall and grips a vertical support. His suit jacket is ripped up the back seam, she notices. And his pants—the cuffs still have mud on them from when it rained last week. She sighs. Evidence that she and her sisters are lousy substitutes for a wife always undoes her. "I bought a book about it," she relents.

"Great," he says. "This is just great." He turns from the wall, smiling.

She remembers supper. "Oh, I've got the burner on high," she cries and runs up to the kitchen.

He follows slowly. Going up and down stairs, he has to hop because of his shot foot. He calls that he's bowled over. "The outlets work?" he calls.

"Yeah, sure."

When he's in the kitchen, he comes up behind her at the stove and drops his hand on her shoulder. "What say we work on it together? This Sunday."

"Sure," she says, stiff under his hand, mortified by love.

On Sunday she rises at six o'clock, when she hears their mother turn on the TV, and does the dusting and two loads of wash so she'll be free the whole day to work with their father. At seven-thirty she puts on the coffee so the aroma will wake him up.

He whistles "For Me and My Gal" in the shower. Norma pours out his Shreddies and orange juice. Feeling benevolent, she takes her plate of toast and jam to eat in the TV room and keep their mother company. A bearded minister is on, saying that everybody's soul is in a constant and everlasting state of torment. Even when you believe yourself to be happy, the minister says, even when you are an innocent, gurgling baby, your soul is contorting in character-building pain. "This is good," he declares. "This is one of life's eternal verities."

"You girls used to skip off to Sunday school holding hands," their mother says wistfully. "That dance skip from the Wizard of Oz. I always hoped you'd turn out like the McGuire sisters."

When Norma hears their father getting dressed, she goes back to the kitchen and pours out his coffee.

He is wearing his navy suit.

"I'm on my way," he says, looking past her to the clock on the wall. "I've got to go into the office."

"Today?"

"No rest for the weary." He is already gone down the hall. Whistling "Easter Parade."

It's still early. Eight-fifteen. Norma eats his cereal, does the dishes, empties out the wastepaper baskets and refills her mother's mug. She washes the kitchen floor. Now it's nine-twenty.

She stands at the window, looking out at their little weeping willow tree that has no leaves left. Its bare branches hanging down make her think of the thin shocked arms of Vietnamese war children, and that makes her hungry. She has a piece of bread. Two pieces, three. Before she knows it, she's devoured almost the whole loaf. She goes downstairs.

It's like a light turning on inside herself to see the fluorescent lights flicker white, all working. She stands there reconsidering how she'll proceed.

"He would have got on your nerves," a voice inside her says. "He'd have taken over and bossed you around. Everything works out for the best."

She holds her breath. She has never heard Jimmy speak to her when she isn't standing in front of where his picture is. After several minutes, while she waits to hear if he has anything else to say, she goes into their father's workroom and takes the photo from the accordion file.

Jimmy's face seems to be straining to communicate an urgent message.

"What?" she asks aloud.

She hears the TV upstairs, the furnace come on. She hears her own thoughts registering these events, and presently she is aware of the fact that the sound of her brother's voice is the sound of herself thinking.

She stares at the picture, taken when he was three months away from going to heaven. She kisses it and puts it away. She is fraught with a sense of having encountered an eternal verity. Returning to the other room, she feels that her legs are heavier and more muscular. And her hand, gripping the hammer, is mighty, and afflicted with responsibility.

At noon she goes up to the kitchen to make lunch. Lou, who came in late last night from babysitting, has just got out of bed. She is still in her pajamas, hunched at the table over a cup of black coffee, smoking their father's cigarettes. Her long hair is tangled and greasy, and her skin is sallow. Seeing her through different eyes, Norma divines that Lou is on the road to becoming a bag lady. "You should give those up," she says about the cigarettes.

"Fuck off," Lou says incredulously. She takes a deep drag. "I gather Giovanni Masturbati is out humping," she says.

Giovanni Masturbati is one of Lou's names for their father. It comes from a dirty song. Lou knows a slew of dirty songs, and lately she sings them as if they're all about their father and Lovergirl. She has decided that one of the greatest things that has ever happened to them is their father having affairs.

Norma spreads margarine on the bread that she didn't polish off a couple of hours ago. "Has Mom had anything to eat?" she asks.

"I gave her a can of beans," Lou says. "She's on some memory lane trip about how cute we used to be going to church."

"Reminiscing is a sign of old age," Norma says sadly, struck by another divination that their mother will die before her time.

Sandy comes into the kitchen, pours herself a cup of coffee and sits across from Lou.

"You've got too much makeup on," Lou says.

"Have I?" Sandy asks quickly, touching her face.

Norma turns from the counter. "Get a load of you," she says.

"Do you think I've got too much on?" Sandy asks her. "Tell me the truth."

The truth, Norma thinks reverently. She looks Sandy over. Hair tied back in a blue ribbon. Tight yellow shell sweater that Sandy knit herself and that makes her breasts appear artificially high and round. Short, hip-hugging, blue-and-yellow-striped skirt. Blue high heels. All blue and yellow to match her eyes and hair. And blue shadow on her eyelids. And false eyelashes? Norma asks.

"Do they look false?" Sandy asks nervously.

"Yes," Norma says. "Yes, I think they do. I don't think you should wear them."

"What's with the opinions all of a sudden?" Lou says. Then she lifts her chin, alert. "Is that in our driveway?"

Sandy stands to see out the window. "Oh, no. Dad's home." She holds up a hand as if he could tell from out there that she's wearing makeup.

"He won't care," Norma says to her.

"I can't take any chances," Sandy says. She runs out to the front hall, runs in again carrying her coat and runs out the back door.

"What the fuck is he doing home?" Lou mutters, getting up to empty the ashtray, waving her hands at the cigarette smoke.

Norma goes to the window. "Something's the matter," she says.

"If he and Lovergirl have split up already, I'll slash my wrists."

"I think he's had a heart attack or something," Norma says.

"What?" Lou flies over beside Norma. He's still in the car, his forehead dropped on the steering wheel. "Shit," Lou whispers. They watch him for a couple of minutes, and he doesn't move. "He's dead," Lou whispers.

He sits up straight.

"Oh, thank heavens," Norma breathes.

"What's he trying to pull?" Lou says angrily.

The car door opens, and he climbs out and stands there surveying the house. His eyes skim past them at the window. His tie is loose, his mouth hanging open.

"God damn it!" Lou says, stamping her bare foot. "They've split up. God fucking damn it!" And then she runs and gets her coat and boots, and heads for the back door, pulling the coat over her pajamas.

"You're going out like *that?*" Norma says.

"I'm sure as hell not hanging around *here* another minute."

One door slams, the other opens. Norma puts her plate in the sink and tiptoes down to the basement. She hears the hangers clink in the hall closet, him walk into the kitchen, the fridge open, the cutlery drawer open, and even—she is so still and vibrant—the release of gas as the beer cap clicks off.

He scrapes back a chair. She's afraid to resume hammering in case he storms down and decides he's mad after all that she started refinishing the basement. Wrecks what she's done. Anything is possible—likely—if he's split up with Lovergirl.

But after a minute the sun comes out and through the window in front of her, striking her smack in the face, and she immediately understands that this is a sign from the source of grace that was Jimmy. A sign to go ahead, to fear not.

She ties on the tool pouch, draws out the hammer and pounds in a nail, and she hears him stand, but it's to get another beer out of the fridge.

A few minutes later he gets a third. Is he going on a binge? Once before, after the breakup with his first Lovergirl, he went on binges for a week or so, on and off between getting into uproars. The binges were as bad as the uproars because he was like a moron when he was plastered, crying, slurring his words, tripping over his feet, like a clown drunk. Even their mother was driven to say that he didn't know his limit.

Another beer. Four. Norma keeps track, her worry rising. She knows his limit: a six pack. And yet it's also happening that as she imagines him up there growing weaker, she is turning into a tower of strength. The sensation is much more vivid than it was in the morning. She is sure that she's taller and that her shirt is suddenly tight around her upper arms. She flexes. Her bicep seems enormous. Hard as a rock. She runs into the laundry room, where on the wall above the sink there is a mirror—a relic from the days that their mother did the wash—and looks at her face. She takes off her glasses, going closer, to see her eyes.

"God," she says, because her eyes aren't shining, huge and glorious, as she imagines Jimmy's eyes would be by now. Her eyes are their father's eyes. Has she always had his eyes, or has this just happened? She puts her glasses back on and goes into the other room, troubled by what having their father's eyes will turn her into. Upstairs he's taking the last beer out of the fridge. She knows how many there are up there. If he wants any more, he'll have to get them out of the old fridge down here.

A few minutes pass, then, *bang*—the empty beer bottle slammed on the table. The search in the fridge for another. The descent, thunderous with his limp and intoxication combined. Her new strength being spiritual as well as physical, she is calm.

He squints, assailed by the new lights. When he can see, he says, "Hey," and plants his hands on his hips. "Alrighty," he says. "Where are we?"

He isn't loaded yet. But his eyes are her eyes gone to hell. They break her heart. "Well," she says, "I've measured most of the wood for that wall, so it just has to be sawn and then it can go up."

"Alrighty." He takes off his jacket and tie. "Give me the saw."

She does, gladly. She lifts a piece of wood onto the table.

"Hold it," he orders, and she grasps the wood close to where she's drawn a line. She exults at the risk to her fingers, the demonstration of her fearlessness and faith. But despite all the beers, he follows the line. He saws steadily and without talking, except to say "Next," one piece of wood after another. All the wood she has measured.

He suggests a break. He gets a beer from the fridge, and his cigarettes and lighter from his jacket pocket, and they sit across from each other on pieces of insulation. Now, smoking, the alcohol shows. His face collapses. He stares off. Out of the blue he begins telling her how he and their mother met, a story Norma already knows. It was during the war. He was a soldier, their mother was a dancer with The Light Fantastics. He was knocked out by her aristocratic ankles and how easily she did the splits. He bribed his way backstage and gave her his kidney stone that he carried everywhere for luck. On their first date they became engaged, the stone serving as a ring until he could afford the real thing.

"She talked her head off," he says. "All the time. Couldn't shut her up. Never drank. Never touched the stuff."

Norma pictures her. A young, blonde, sober chatterbox in those tap shoes she still has, clicking them as she walks, wearing the feather hat from the newspaper picture.

"You'd have thought that's when she'd have started," their father says.

"Started what?"

He raises his beer, meaning started drinking. "Both brothers dying within a week."

"In battle," Norma says, to prompt him to tell her more. All she knows about her uncles is that they were older than their mother and that one was named Jim, the same as their father, and one was named Archie. When the second one, Jim, died, their mother's father, who was named James Archibald and who won a medal in the First World War, went out to his barn and shot a sow, then wouldn't let anybody butcher it for meat. This story Norma has heard before from their father. Their mother won't talk about her brothers dying.

"Think I'll call it quits," their father says, pulling himself up. He goes to the fridge for as many beers as he can carry, and takes them upstairs.

Which means he'll conk out before dinner, probably until the morning. Which means he won't get into an uproar, not tonight at least.

Sandy is half an hour early. A black car is parked in a corner, but it isn't Reg's. Reg drives a red Mustang. Friday evening when she arrived at the store, there was an envelope stamped "Confidential," and with her name on it, next to the cash register. The note inside was typed on Sherman "Sher-fit" Shoes letterhead. "Doll," it said. "Re Sunday. One p.m. Glenn Mills High parking lot. Red mustang. See you there! Reg."

She woke up Friday morning thinking no way could she date a man who was only eight years younger than their father, but the note changed her mind because of the trouble he'd gone to . . . typing it, using his good office paper. Also she was taken with "Doll."

She knows what's going to happen. In her body she knows. Shivers pour through her. At work she went weak in the knees when one of the salesgirls said you should never throw water on mating dogs, because the male dog's thing makes a hook inside the female, and the female is torn if the male pulls out before his thing goes down.

A red car roars into the lot and accelerates. For a second, before the brakes squeal, she's sure it's going to run her down.

Reg leans across the seat and opens the passenger door. Music blares. Frank Sinatra singing "That's Life." When she gets in, he turns it down a bit. He's wearing black leather driving gloves, new-looking blue jeans and a black leather jacket. "A puppet, a poet, a pauper, a pirate, a pawn and a king," he sings to her. His eyes zigzag over her face, making the cross-stitch. She asks where they're going.

"Anywhere but here," he says, turning the radio back up.

Sandy hates Frank Sinatra because their father has all his albums, and she associates him with their father's secret life—ladies who are tramps, cigarette smoke, drinks and laughs. She wishes Reg would change the station or at least turn the volume back down. Call her "Doll," make her glad she's come. He drives fast and mouths the words hugely over at her: "I just-uh pick myself up and get-uh back in the race."

She folds her arms and looks out her window, and he switches the radio right off. His right hand drops on her thigh. "Baby, baby, baby," he says consolingly, giving her a squeeze.

A current goes through her, up from his hand. Continuing to give her little squeezes, he says that she looks good enough to eat, that she makes his mouth water, that he has a yen for her. She lays her head on the soft leather of his shoulder, and the road flying under them is her life until this moment.

When they are out of traffic, he doesn't waste time. "Take off your coat," he says in the same businessman's voice that he told her to meet him in the doughnut shop.

She obeys.

"Lift up the sweater," he says, turning the car heater to high. "Slow. Nice and slow," he says in a voice to demonstrate.

She inches her sweater up. Below her breasts she pauses. She is inspired to pause there as if out of shyness. But although she has never shown her breasts to anyone, not even let her sisters see them since she's developed, she isn't feeling shy.

She has on a pink bra, trimmed in lace daisies. As she draws her sweater to her shoulders, she watches his eyes race from her to the road to her. She knows that his yen is for her white skin and how young she is.

They're in the country now. He pulls into a laneway that flames with sumac and cuts the engine but keeps the heater on. Over the gear shift he kisses her.

For a few minutes they neck, softly, their bodies not touching. He continues to grip the steering wheel, and she is beginning to wonder if anything else is going to happen when he clamps his hand between her legs. Her heart seems to shake her whole body. She thinks that his hand must feel how she shakes. He rubs back and forth, and then, keeping his gloves on, he curls his fingers under her pants and strokes her lightly with his knuckles. She likes that. She shifts closer and puts her arms around his neck. She moans. And simultaneously feels a sharp pain that has her tearing away from his mouth and that she thinks is pure cruelty until he withdraws his hand, looks at his index and middle fingers, shows them to her, and she sees they are smeared wet. Her blood.

"The gates of heaven are now open," he says.

He has her remove her bra and underpants and straddle his middle, facing him, the driver's seat pushed back as far as it will go. He grasps his penis so that it's pointing straight up. In case it makes her lose her nerve, she doesn't look down.

"Sit on it, baby," he groans.

She raises herself and comes down in slow motion. He guides himself in. She thinks of her vagina as he said—as a pearly gate—and his penis as a battering ram. All the small bones inside her seem to be splintering. Her eyes water from the pain. His eyes, his old eyes, are squeezed shut as if it hurts him, too.

Once she is all the way down, he holds her by the waist and moves her slowly up again, then down. Her insides make room. His eyes open and plant on her breasts. She notices that the moles on his bald spot make a *J*. Out of relief that she isn't really hurting any longer, she kisses the *J*. He kisses her breasts. He moves her up and down again. Again, faster, deeper. She cries out at the knifing pain. He says, "Oh baby, oh baby, oh baby," jiggles her breasts, and throws his head back, eyes shut. His penis deflates inside her, in a hot pool.

He is gasping as if he's run for his life. She is leaking blood all over his new blue jeans, but he doesn't care. Beads of sweat ring his hairline. She touches them, a little awed by all the physical eruptions. She curls into his chest, and he strokes her back. She is his little puppy, his little baby.

Off and on for two weeks their father is drunk. In his sober spells, in the mornings and after work, the girls keep expecting a tantrum that never comes. He hardly even speaks to them. He stands at windows, gazing out.

When it appears that the binge is over, Lou says, "I give this heartbroken humper act another twenty-four hours."

But days, weeks pass, and he stays gloomy and lost to the world. One night Lou says "shit" at the breakfast table and gets away with it.

He really doesn't seem to be looking for trouble.

The only thing he's interested in is refinishing the basement.

After supper he looks over at Norma as if it's all hopeless but what the hell and asks, does she want to put in a few hours? He has apparently forgotten about her study regime.

He has big plans. A stone fireplace and a bedroom for himself. A four-piece bathroom. A wet bar. So before they can go on with the insulating, they have to tackle the plumbing. As they work, he describes what they're doing and why. He doesn't like her to interrupt with questions. In fact, the one time he is the least bit short with her is when she asks him something.

Otherwise, he is even-tempered and not at all bossy. He lets her solder. She believes that he trusts her and wants her around him because Jimmy's spirit is radiating out of her and striking him unawares. She feels that he's especially affected after he's had a few beers.

The truth is, he isn't a hundred percent on the wagon. Sometimes, once a week maybe, he stops working, gets a beer out of the fridge and sits on the floor drinking it and three or four more while she carries on, if she can, at what they've been doing. He gazes at her, frowning, as if he's noticed something different about her but can't put his finger on it. And then, suddenly, he gets up and joins her again. What she thinks is that it's her strength that he's noticed and can't put his finger on, and it's Jimmy's spirit that compels him to stop drinking and get back to work.

One evening after drinking for a while, he empties down the laundry tubs all the beer that's in the fridge. Then he strokes her hair and says it is so shiny, so healthy, but she should let it grow.

For the next few weeks she feels as if she has entered another golden period of her life. Most of the time, even at school, she is elated. On top of basking in her magical strength and radiance, she can't get it out of her mind, their father stroking her hair. He has never done anything like that before. As she lies in bed at night, she thinks about it.

One night she just has to tell Lou about him stroking her hair. Lou is reading in bed, and Norma, looking at her sister's small head and her long dark hair falling like a veil, wishes that their father would lay his hand on Lou's head, too, that the whole family would experience his benediction.

"Don't make me puke," is Lou's response.

Norma sighs. What did she expect? And yet she concentrated all her being into pouring a river of goodness out of her eyes. Why wasn't Lou affected? She asks Lou if she ever thinks about their brother.

A pause. "No." Lou returns to her book.

"I found a picture of him."

Lou narrows her eyes. "Where?"

"Downstairs. Under Dad's workbench."

"What did he look like?"

"A baby. Me as a baby."

Lou is silent, frowning at her book, but Norma can tell that she isn't reading. And although Norma knows better than to go on, her eyes are full with a yearning that she thinks must be the urging of heaven, so she tells Lou everything. About hearing Jimmy's voice emanating from his picture. About asking his advice. About the day when she felt as if she had become Jimmy . . . as if Jimmy had entered her. "My thoughts and feelings," she says, "half the time they feel like his. Even my body feels like his."

Lou speaks at last. "*Your* body is a boy's," she says flatly.

"I mean his strength."

Lou slaps shut her book. "You know what you're telling me?"

Norma waits.

"You're telling me that you're a schizophrenic."

"No! No, I'm not two different people. I'm one person in two persons. Like the holy trinity is God in three persons."

"I just hope Dad's got the dough for a shrink. That's all I hope."

"I'm not a schizophrenic!" Norma says, almost shouting. Automatically she listens for their father, forgetting for a second that he isn't yelling these days. Then she says, "It happens to people all the time with Jesus. Jesus enters their hearts. His light is in them, guiding them. Well, it's Jimmy who entered my heart."

"What makes you think he was a big saint? Christ, he was only just born when he died. He was a baby. He shit, he ate, he slept."

Norma falls on her side, facing the wall. "Just forget it," she says.

"*You* forget it," Lou says, switching off the lights between their beds. "Another goddamn crazy person in this house is all I need."

When Lou baby sits, she warns the kids to stay out of her hair. Then she shuts herself up in one of the rooms and does her homework and smokes cigarettes, the parents' if there's a pack lying around. When her homework is done, she reads dirty magazines and books. Most of the houses she goes to regularly have at least *Playboy* magazines stashed away somewhere. If the house has bookcases, something mildly trashy might be on the top shelf or behind the rows, out of sight. The hard-core paperbacks are under chair cushions, under workbenches. You have to know where to look.

Her curiosity is mainly for what these pillars of the community go in for. To discover favorite passages she lets books fall open. She commits entire pages to memory for reciting to Sherry, who is never surprised.

"I know the type," Sherry says.

Sherry has slept with so many guys that she says her vagina can't hold in a tampon.

Lou, on the other hand, is still a virgin, because boys aren't interested in her. They think of her as a kid, despite a padded bra that provides her with high, pointed breasts that never fail to startle and rivet *her* when she catches sight of her reflection.

She babysits a fat six-month-old boy who is always flopping his face into her chest and trying to suckle her caved-in bra. "Foreplay," she jokes to Sherry.

The sex part is rubbing a prescription cream, smelling of cherry cough drops, on the baby's penis.

On Lou's first afternoon babysitting him, his mother, late for a curling match, wearing a plaid tam and clomping around in big curling boots, whips the baby onto the change table, trains the floor lamp on him, unpins his diaper, and there in the spotlight is the first human penis Lou has ever laid eyes on.

"Okay, imagine it ten times as big but with the balls about the same size they are now," Sherry says later.

The baby's inflammation is from urine catching in the foreskin. "I guess I should've had him circumcised," the mother confesses in a frazzled tone.

She has Lou apply the cream. From the tip down. Rubbing it in until it isn't visible, then putting on another coat. Meanwhile the baby kicks as if he intends injury.

In November the mother enters a spree of curling tournaments and hires Lou to come over two afternoons from four until six and on Sundays from noon 'til five. It's easy money. The kid hardly ever cries and then only for a few minutes and an obvious reason, like dropping his bottle. Sometimes he gurgles or smiles at her, and she wants to pick him up and cuddle him, but whenever she does, he goes straight for one of her breasts. After a few times babysitting him, she doesn't find this funny anymore. "Fat glutton," she says impatiently, thinking of Norma. If she holds him away from her chest, he squirms and thrashes and turns beet red in the face. So she stops picking him up at all unless she has to. She puts him in his Bathinette on one end of the dining-room table and does her homework at the other end.

The normal life in other people's houses she finds soothing. Conducive to study. Out of pride and contrariety she studies hard on the sly. Nobody expects her to be so smart—not the teachers who give her detentions for absence and talking back, not the other students who think she's a loser for hanging around with a tramp, not even the tramp, who thinks she only reads porn.

On nice days Lou takes the baby over to Sherry's. Outside of his house he strikes her as almost freakishly fat and stupid-looking. She races the carriage and lets it fly ahead of her. A playground is beside Sherry's apartment, and she and Sherry bring him down to it, and Lou pushes his swing so high it's parallel with the bars. Sherry screams. Up in her bedroom Sherry bounces him gently on her knee and plays pat-a-cake. He doesn't squirm with Sherry. He seems to like her.

"Oh, I want one," she whines.

"Say the word," Lou says, holding Sherry's diaphragm over the wastepaper basket.

One day when Sherry picks the baby up, and he starts mouthing the front of her blouse, she says she heard about a woman who adopted a baby and was able to nurse it because its sucking got her milk hormones working.

"Be my guest," Lou says.

So Sherry undoes her blouse and black push-up bra and pokes a huge brown nipple into his mouth. He sucks noisily. Every time they check, though, there's no milk. She tries the other nipple, but it doesn't work either.

"I guess being felt up all the time confuses your hormones," Sherry sighs. She wants Lou to try.

"No way." Lou is repulsed at the thought. She snatches the baby from Sherry and throws him on the bed.

"You've broken his neck," Sherry cries, because he is silent.

"He's okay," Lou says, bending over him. His eyes are unblinking. "If looks could kill," she says. She holds his gaze. She wonders whether he'll have any memory of this when he's the six-foot-five, three-hundred-pound guy she's sure he'll be, given his appetite. He won't know why, but he'll hate skinny, dark-haired girls. She wonders if their brother, Jimmy, was like him. If all babies are like him (he's the only one she babysits). "How are you supposed to love them," she says, "when they don't love you back?"

"They love you," Sherry protests. "They love anyone who looks after them."

"That's not love, that's survival instinct."

"Well, that's what so lovable about them. How helpless they are."

"That's not lovable," Lou says.

To make herself a worthier vessel of Jimmy, Norma goes on a diet and in a month loses fifteen pounds. By then her hair is long enough to tie back with an elastic band. That's how she prefers it—brushed away from her face, appearing short from the front.

Her friends turn on her. The tall girl says that her legs are too thin for her body now, that when she was heavier, her body was in better proportion. The girl with acne says, "If I had a widow's peak, I sure wouldn't show it off." And "All you think about is yourself."

While it's true that Norma thinks a lot about who she is, it isn't true that she puts herself before others. Always chiming through her head are Jimmy's commandments to be kind. She never worried much about hurting her friends before, but she worries now. In spite of which she occasionally gives them the slip and walks down the corridors by herself, looking at pretty girls. She feels humbly entitled. She feels that God might grant her, who is not beautiful but who is moved by beauty, at least the pleasure of looking.

But it would never occur to her to change herself to attract pretty girls. Her weight loss is entirely for her brother, to house his spirit, and her longer hair is for their father. The fact that she is becoming more attractive to the rest of the world is so incidental that she doesn't realize it. Nobody tells her.

Although their father doesn't mention her hair again, she feels that he is well pleased with her for how she slaps tools in his palm like an operating-room nurse and for being a good listener. As they work, he tells stories about when he was boy nicknamed Jumbo on account of his big ears, which Grandma Field boxed at least once a day for good measure. He says that just like Sandy he used to like resting his ear on an empty dinner plate. As they work, he is full of these surprising facts.

Away from the rec room, however, around the rest of the family, he is still gloomy and quiet. He forgets to buy a Christmas tree, and finally, on December 24, Lou arrives home with a bent, pathetic little spruce that she dug up from someone's lawn.

"If we're lucky," she says, "he'll forget to buy us gifts, too."

He doesn't. He gets them all out-of-style green-and-blue-plaid parkas, and for Lou and Sandy he also gets out-of-style patterned knee-socks.

Norma's second gift is a red angora sweater.

"Gee, that's not bad," Sandy says in an amazed, envious voice.

"Try it on," their father suggests, spreading his arms across the back of the chesterfield.

It's too small. Norma knew it would be as soon as she saw it, but she goes into her bedroom and puts it on anyway. She can hardly glance at herself in the mirror. Big, disgusting. Screaming red. She tears the sweater off.

Why red? She never wears bright colors. And she never wears anything tight, he must notice that. She stands there pulling the sweater in and out like an accordion. She want to cry, thinking of him buying it especially for her. Why didn't he buy her a hammer?

"How's it look?" he calls.

"Great."

"C'mon out. Let's see."

"Okay, just a minute." She puts the sweater back on and walks down the hall feeling as she does as school—that her breasts are hideous and offensive but the shield of her soul.

"Holy shit," Lou says.

Norma looks at their father. "It's really nice," she murmurs.

"Well," he says, nodding. "It seems to fit all right."

His eyes are flitting all over her. She feels sorry for him. She feels that her embarrassment must be nothing compared to his.

Yet he wants her to wear the sweater. On Boxing Day he asks where it is.

"In my dresser," she answers, bewildered. She can't conceive that he's asking why the sweater isn't on her back. Actually, it's in Sandy's dresser. She's given it to Sandy.

"What are you saving it for?" he asks. "Go put it on."

"Now?"

"Sure. Why not?"

"Aren't we working on the rec room today?"

"A little sawdust never hurt anything."

She figures that he can't stand the idea of all the money he spent going to waste (Sandy thinks the sweater cost at least twenty dollars), that he can't face the fact that he's made an expensive mistake. If he's prepared to accept her in the sweater, Norma knows she should be, too. But when she puts it on, she is unable to leave the bedroom. At last she pulls a cardigan on over top and leaves the buttons at the neck open to show the sweater's turtleneck. He doesn't say anything.

That day and during the rest of the Christmas holidays they finish the bathroom. To make him happy, she wears the sweater under her work shirt or under the cardigan. On the last day (a precarious day, being the last, because when they complete any job he is liable to say, "This calls for a celebration," and then down a six pack) he has a chest cold and turns the furnace way up, causing them both to perspire. He insists she remove her shirt when she wipes her forehead on the tail of it.

"You don't need all those layers," he says.

Part of her feels released. He is telling her that he doesn't care what she looks like. Oh, to be taken for granted! But she can't take herself for granted, not in that sweater. She hunches and folds her arms.

When the last tile is down on the floor, sure enough he begins drinking. She stays with him like the angel on his shoulder, occupying herself by sitting at the little laundry table beside the fridge and taking all the screws out of the screw and nail box and sorting them. He watches her and drinks in silence.

In the middle of beer five he walks over to her. Bending forward, he reaches across in front of her, and his hand bumps against her breasts.

She stiffens. Their eyes meet, and she has the positive, unearthly feeling that he's touched her on purpose.

"Sorry," he mutters. What he's reaching for is the hammer that's lying beside the box on her far side. He gets the hammer and his beer, and dragging his bad leg, crosses to the end wall. After many attempts he yanks out a crooked nail in one of the beams.

"Jesus bids us shine with a pure, clear light," Norma thinks frantically, as a kind of cleansing prayer. She is overcome with shame. Her filthy mind. Across the room, his back to her, their father runs his palm over the beam, his arm going in and out of a dusty, sallow wedge of sunlight.

What is God's idea of pure clear? she wonders. How much contamination does He make allowances for?

Tuesday evenings at six-thirty and Sunday afternoons at one, Reg picks Sandy up at the bus stop. Luckily their father doesn't pay attention to her comings and goings.

After sex, Reg lies back panting and says, "I'm a broken man." Then he has a cigarette and talks about the shoe business or about the hell he went through when he was married to his first wife, "the dyke."

His second wife, the one he has now, is a great mother and a great party thrower, but he's pretty sure she's turning into a dyke, too, because she's gone off intercourse.

"She's probably happy you've got a girlfriend," Sandy volunteers.

"Are you out of your mind?" he says.

They always drive to the old motel strip on the two-lane highway going into the city. So as not to leave an obvious trail, they change motels each time, and about a block away from the one he's decided on, Sandy gets out of the car to let him drive ahead and check in alone. The Mustang is usually the only car in the parking lot. How do these places stay in business? she wonders. Reg tries to get the highest-numbered room, but sometimes, who knows why, he can't and has to whisper-yell at her from the door—opened a crack—as she walks past. It isn't just his wife that worries him. It's that Sandy is jailbait, and he wants to be able to claim, if he has to, that she propositioned him.

In the room there are a few lonely moments during which he paces in his overcoat and says that he has a feeling the desk clerk recognized him from the store, or that his wife knows something fishy is going on. Sandy wanders into the bathroom and turns on the light that is also a fan. The perfection of her face in the mirror comforts her. It gives her the composure to sit like a lady on the edge of his bed until he stops pacing and sits beside her.

She does whatever he likes. She tries to anticipate it. Except to make him happy, she has no desires herself, but she's good at guessing his. On their third date he is lying on his back after making love, and she kisses the line of black hair on his stomach all the way down to his penis, kisses the tip of his penis, and just knows that what he wants is for her to put the whole thing in her mouth.

"Oh, yeah, baby," he says when she does.

He covers her ears with his hands and moves her head up and down. She thinks they've invented something. His ejaculation is like the dentist's squirter except warmer and tasting of salt and Javex.

"You can swallow it," he gasps.

She already has.

The day that he breaks off with her, she guesses he is going to the minute she climbs into the car. Something tells her, she couldn't say what. Leaning against the passenger door, feeling nothing, she waits. Even when they drive to the motel strip and pull over onto the shoulder, as usual, she knows she isn't supposed to hop out.

In silence they both watch the traffic. It seems a quarter of an hour passes before he speaks.

"My wife knows."

"Oh."

"She went nuts. Completely out of her mind. Crying, screaming. . . ."

Sandy regards her white hands with the eyes of his wife, who she imagines has age spots and dishpan hands. A woman almost as old as their mother. Out of her mind. When their father made them pin their mother to the bed, their mother cried and screamed. In the hallway, Norma held on to her, strong as a man.

"But how did she find out?" Sandy asks.

"I told her." He sighs. "She knew something was up. I said I had to see you one more time. To break it off. Christ Almighty—" He shakes his head, laughs bitterly. "She wanted to come along." He runs his fingers over the top of his head, as if he still has hair. Sandy thinks he looks really old. She can't imagine having kissed him, let alone the rest. She closes her eyes.

"Ah, baby," he says. "Ah, baby doll, I'm sorry." His hand drops on her thigh. "I was going to tell you after we boogie-woogied." She opens her eyes. He is smiling sappily at her. "God, you know, you could wear me down yet. Right here. This minute. One last time." He strokes her leg and brings his mouth to her ear. "Say the word," he whispers. "I'm a weak man."

A bus is coming down the road. If she runs, she can catch it. She picks up her purse, opens the door and gets out.

"I'll drive you," he shouts, his voice falling away.

On Tuesday evening she happens to glance at the kitchen clock at exactly six-thirty—the time she usually meets him—and her heart starts hammering, then seems to stop dead. She places her hand over it and can't feel a beat. It reminds her of trying to feel the heartbeat of the Santa Claus man, and it occurs to her that maybe he wasn't dead after all. That seems like a dream, that day. Nothing has ever felt so lovely as when she had her feet in his lap and he stroked them with a blade of grass.

The next morning as she stands in her slip surveying the contents of her closet, she thinks, What does it matter what I wear? Since meeting Reg, she has stopped dating boys from school. Their soft hands and pink lips disgust her. They are just tall six-year-olds, unsophisticated, loud-mouthed. If one of them goes to bed with a girl, the whole school knows about it.

"Oh, Reg," she sighs, pulling down any old dress from its hanger. But she doesn't cry.

It takes about a week for her to realize that whenever she thinks of something specific about Reg, apart from his laugh and their love-making, for instance if she thinks of his bald spot or the clumps of black hair on his back or him singing Frank Sinatra songs, she is relieved that she won't be seeing him again. There's a hole in her life, but it's a hole that can be filled by another nice, well-dressed gentleman. Such as Bob, the Englishman who drives a Mercedes and picked her up at the bus stop a couple of weeks ago and took her all the way to work.

"I'm dating someone," she told him.

"Here's my card," he said.

The card is pale blue with silver lettering: Robert Featherstone, President, Featherstone and Ridley Corp. Two weeks after she and Reg break up, she calls him from a phone booth, and they make a date for the next evening.

He takes her to his office on the seventeenth floor of a new bank building downtown. "Let's just say I play Monopoly for real," he says when she asks him what he does. On a white wall-to-wall shag carpet they make love in their clothes, him still in his coat, getting inside her by tugging her underpants out of the way. Before they leave his office, he writes her initials beside seven o'clock on Thursday in his appointment book.

Since she works Thursday nights, she has to phone in sick, something she's never done before. "It's that goddamn Asiatic flu," Mrs. Dart says sympathetically. She prescribes hot toddies.

Bob picks Sandy up at the same bus stop where she used to wait for

Reg. As soon as she gets in his car, he slips his hand up to her underpants and hooks a finger around the crotch.

"I've got to pop in at the office," he says in his voice like Rex Harrison's.

His finger stays hooked. She can't shift position or think of anything to say. "I've caught a little fish," he says at a stoplight. All the way downtown he holds on. Even when they park, he doesn't let go immediately, and she has a few seconds of terror that he's a pervert, that he's going to try to pull her by her underpants out of the car and down the street.

But of course he doesn't. When he releases her, she feels stupid for having thought something so crazy about the president of a company.

At his office she walks in ahead of him over to his desk. He shuts and locks the door, and the next thing she knows, he lifts her skirt up and presses himself into her rear end. He already has an erection. They make love standing there. He grasps her by the waist, and she rests her forearms on his green leather desk pad. There's a handwritten airmail letter at right angles to her line of vision. "Dear Bobbo," she reads before he covers the rest with his hand.

"Use this," he says when she reaches for a piece of foolscap to catch the semen dripping out of her. He tosses a clean white linen handkerchief on the desk.

"Are you sure?" she asks, thinking of his wife on laundry day.

"I have a bit of work to do," he says.

"That's okay. I'll wait out at the reception." Holding the handkerchief between her legs, she turns to face him.

His hands are praying under his chin. "No," he says slowly. "No. You see, I shall be an hour at least."

"Oh." From his saying he was only "popping in" at the office, she assumed that they were going somewhere else, to a motel, that this didn't count.

"Be a good girl and go on down," he says. "I'll ring you a taxi." He takes a couple of bills out of his wallet and gives them to her, retrieving his handkerchief at the same time.

The bills are twenties. "This is way too much," she says.

"Keep the change," he says. He doesn't check his appointment book for a night to fit her in.

. . .

Their father gives up on the basement. If he comes home at all, he leaves again right after supper. He doesn't have a new Lovergirl, though. There's no sign of that.

Their mother seems to get it into her head that what's the matter with him is serious enough to demand her reserves. Since the bomb shelter she has eaten all her meals in front of the TV, but the morning after their father stops working on the rec room, she takes it upon herself to turn up at the breakfast table. She has combed her long white hair and bobby-pinned it behind her ears, and she is wearing a green cinch belt around her housecoat, which almost makes it look as if she's gotten dressed.

Throughout the meal she carries on wifely chatter, speaking more in half an hour than she has in a month. It doesn't work, and even Lou can see that it's not his fault. "As long as Harold doesn't grab the limelight," their mother says at one point, pouring milk into coffee that their father now takes black, referring to a man, who, it turns out, is Arnold, not Harold, and who left where their father works five years ago. So then their mother says, laughing, "Where does the time fly?" and then she looks out the window and asks whose car that is in the driveway. "But yours isn't white, Jim," she protests. He stands up to leave. Straightening her out could take all day.

Still, Lou, stung by their mother's pathetic effort, says, "What a creep" when he's gone.

Their mother slowly draws the bobby pins out of her hair. "He's blue," she says.

"So what?"

"He's got the blues," their mother rephrases, her eyes drifting off.

As far as the rec room is concerned, Norma goes on putting up the panelling by herself. But she's worried about their father. What should I do? she wonders until her inner voice answers.

"Go to church," it says.

She hasn't been inside a church in ten years. She decides to go to the Catholic church rather than to the one her family belongs to — the Presbyterian — for it seems to her that God pays more attention to Catholics. On her knees in front of rows of candles she appeals to the huge painting on the wall of the Christ child floating in Mary's arms.

"Help my father," she prays. "If he saw the look of suspicion in my eyes when he bumped into me, please, please tell him he didn't really see it."

Weeks pass. Sometimes as she prays she feels her heart race. She feels that this is the spirit of the baby brother inside her exalting at the sight of the baby Jesus on the wall. At home she keeps her hair clean and brushed and returns to her study regime. She even wears the red sweater on its own once.

When their father comes downstairs for a beer, one evening at about nine o'clock, she thinks that her prayers have been answered. As far as she knows, he hasn't been in the basement since he stopped working with her. He seems tired but pent up. He opens the beer and comes over to where she is sawing.

"I thought I'd finish off the paneling," she says shyly. She notices that he needs to go to the barber's. His brush cut is slanting like dead winter grass. When he looks a mess is when she loves him so much that she can hardly breathe.

"Have you lost weight?" he asks, frowning at her.

"A bit," she says, in case that's what he's frowning about. In fact, she's lost twenty-two pounds.

He cocks his head and squints at her. "How old are you? Nineteen?"

"Eighteen."

"How would you like me to teach you to drive?"

She stares at him. "Really?"

"Why not?" He takes a swig of beer. "Time you learned."

"But—" She lets out a breath. Where is his memory? He's said that he'd never let any of them drive his car, that girls shouldn't drive. "Well, okay," she says. "Sure."

His lips tighten into a smile.

"I'm pissed off," Lou tells the baby. The baby kicks the tube out of her hand. "Can't say I blame you," Lou sighs and decides not to apply the cream today. It doesn't seem to be doing any good; his penis is as red as the first time she babysat him. She feels a little sorry for him—a raw thumb between his legs, a mother too busy to get him a better prescription. Too busy to find him a nice babysitter.

She repins his diaper and puts him in his Bathinette at one end of the dining-room table. Then she sits at the other end to do her homework. But she can't concentrate, she's too pissed off. This morning, while she was still sleeping, their father took Norma out for a driving lesson. Lou couldn't believe it. She said she wanted to learn how to drive, too, but their father said, "Just Norma." It didn't matter what argument Lou presented, even the peerless one that she needed to drive to do the grocery shopping, he wouldn't give in.

"What if I learn from somebody else?" she asked at last. "Can I at least borrow the car sometimes?"

He shook his head.

"That's not fair!" she screamed and kept screaming it, holding out her arms to block his way to the basement. The vein in his temple began to throb, but instead of backing off, Lou screamed louder.

When he hit her across the side of the head, a look of recognition passed between them, the breaking point being their old rendezvous. Then he shoved past her. She marched down the hall to her and Norma's bedroom.

Norma was sitting at the vanity, brushing her hair. Her glasses were off, and Lou, her ear still ringing, was bothered by how grown-up and attractive Norma looked. Like a foreigner, with her brushed-back dark hair and round face. An Eastern European woman. Exotic and persecuted.

Addressing Lou's reflection in the mirror, Norma said, apologetically, "I'm the oldest."

"So?" Lou said. "I'm old enough to drive."

"You know how he is about girls driving," Norma said, gathering her hair into a ponytail and pulling it through an elastic band. "It's hard enough on him letting me drive."

"So why is he?"

"I don't know. Maybe because of all the work I've done on the basement."

"Bullshit." Lou knew that Norma didn't believe this either. When had their father ever handed out rewards? "Bull fucking shit," Lou said.

Norma gave her a long-suffering look.

The baby is crying. He has somehow managed to twist the blanket around his neck.

"If you'd just lie still," Lou says, lifting his head to unwind the blanket, "nothing would happen to you." He glares at her, then squeezes shut his eyes as if he can't stand what he sees.

They end up pulled over onto the shoulder, the car running to keep the heater on, him drinking a beer, both of them looking through barbed-wire fencing at snowy fields ringed with black, bare trees. The sky is always overcast on these days, which Norma imagines is heaven sympathizing with him. All sorts of ideas enter her mind as she and their father sit there. She thinks, who can say that everything you see isn't a message from God? She grants their father the message of the whole sky, because she has prayed so hard for him and because she feels that the big things would be reserved for men who get as unhappy and as happy as he does.

She is pretty sure that he's teaching her to drive without wanting to, that God put the plan in his head to throw them back into each other's company and to patch up any misunderstandings.

But their father is fighting the setup. It's obvious he'd rather be driving around with his last Lovergirl. He gazes out the passenger window and sighs. He hardly gives Norma any instructions except to tell her which way to turn. He doesn't pay attention to her at all, really, unless she takes a corner too fast or hits the brakes too hard, and then he says, a little annoyed but as if it doesn't matter, "Easy," or "Slow down," or he leans over and steers for a few seconds himself.

She hasn't understood until these drives just how depressed he is. Drinking too much isn't nearly as explicit a sign as not worrying about his car, or—this is probably even more explicit—not worrying about breaking the law.

"Naw, we'll stick to the back roads," he says when she mentions going to get her learner's permit.

Another sign: he doesn't talk. When they were working on the basement, he talked all the time, until he started drinking. In the car, though, he's the same as he is upstairs in the house. Taking his silence as her challenge, Norma tries to start conversations, but he closes his eyes and says "Shhh," as if she's interrupted some complicated or precious thought. He has her drive way out into the country and park on a concession road while he goes through at least a six pack.

In the cafeteria at school Sandy hears a girl say that Lou's friend Sherry is a nymphomaniac for sleeping with guys she doesn't know.

"That's not what a nymphomaniac is," another girl says. "A nymphomaniac is someone who never has a climax."

Either definition fits Sandy. She almost bursts into tears right there. She runs into the washroom and makes a promise to herself to ignore any man who flirts with her.

Eventually she feels clean. Not white clean, but no longer black. She's really lonely, though. She couldn't say for sure that Reg was in love with her, and she knows that Bob wasn't, but when they wanted her so badly that they couldn't wait to get her clothes off, she sure felt loved.

To avoid running into Reg, she has started taking her coffee breaks in a greasy spoon across the street from the fabric store. There's a man who always seems to come into the restaurant the same time she does, and whenever she looks up from her fashion magazine, he's smiling at her. He has gray hair at the temples, wears expensive suits, and laughs and jokes with the waitresses.

One day he saunters over to her table.

"I'm trying to read," she says. He sits down across from her anyway. She looks into his rugged, friendly face and gets a whiff of his manly aftershave.

His name is Rob. The cross between "Reg" and "Bob" doesn't escape her. After work that evening they go to the Nap-a-Wile motel, which she recommends for its vibrating beds. He sticks breath mints up her vagina and fishes them out with his tongue. He tickles her and tells her jokes. Everything strikes him as funny, even intercourse. "I'm having a hell of a good time," he laughs as he enters her.

So is she.

Since he's a traveling salesman for an aluminum company, he can see her pretty well whenever he wants. That's two or three times a week. From the towns he visits during the day he brings her postcards with dirty jokes on them. Sandy is flattered to be treated like a grown woman.

In March he and his wife go to Florida for ten days, and Sandy misses him like crazy. The night he returns, they make love three times. Afterward, in the car, he asks her what she thinks of swinging.

It sounds familiar. She thinks it has to do with sex, but she's not sure what. "I don't know," she answers.

"I've got a twin brother," he says. "He wants to meet you."

She figures he's changing the subject. "An identical twin?" she asks.

He laughs. "You prefer that?"

When he picks her up for their next date, two of him are in the car. The one in the passenger seat gets out. "Hi, I'm Ron," he says in Rob's voice, throwing an arm around her. He points to a purple peanut-shaped birthmark on his chin. "The only difference," he says.

But she notices another difference—Ron isn't wearing a wedding band.

She sits in the front seat, between them. She feels like a mirror. "You're even going gray the same," she says, looking back and forth. On either side of her there is roaring laughter.

They drive to the Nap-a-Wile. Out of the trunk Ron produces a case of beer and a bottle of sherry with a white ribbon on it, "for the lady," leaving her with no choice but to accept the glass he pours when they are in the motel room. She has never drunk sherry before, or wine, or even beer, which Rob knows. It's gentlemanly of him, she thinks, not to give her away. He sits beside her on the edge of the bed, and Ron stands across from them, leaning against the desk. The two brothers tell jokes, supplying each other's punch lines and laughing the same rip-roaring, head-thrown-back laugh. She laughs at the amazingness of being with two Robs.

Is she the only one drinking sherry? The bottle is half empty, but she can't remember filling her glass. Sherry tastes like Lou's friend who is named after it. It tastes way better than what she remembers whiskey tasting like.

That reminds her. "Tell Ron the joke—" She giggles. "Tell him the joke about the drunk lady who thinks the naked man is a cigarette machine."

"Hey, free hand lotion," Ron says.

"You know it!" she cries, laughing. It's *her* joke, one Reg told her, and she only told Rob a couple of days ago.

"'Fraid he knows them all," Rob says, putting his arm around her.

She laughs into his shoulder. "Free hand lotion," she says. She can't stop laughing.

Rob pulls her down onto the bed and starts kissing her all over her face.

"Rob," she laughs. She attempts to sit up.

"It's okay," he says. He pins her down by the shoulders. She stops laughing. "We're going to have a great time," he says, undoing the top button of her blouse.

He undoes all her buttons. She lies perfectly still, chained to his smiling eyes. Then he begins rubbing her breasts, and she comes to and rolls away from him. He catches her arm. "Your brother's watching," she whispers.

His brother laughs. "Hey, go right ahead," he says. "Don't mind me."

"Come on, baby," Rob pleads. Baby—that's new, from him. She sinks into the bed and lets him kiss her on the mouth, and almost forgets that they aren't alone, until his hand slides up her leg.

"I can't," she says, turning her face away.

"Don't do this to me," he says. He sounds so strange and unfriendly that she has an alarming thought.

"Are you Ron?" she whispers.

"What if I was?"

She draws away from him.

"Hey, hey, relax. You know your Uncle Rob, don't you?" He strokes her cheek with the backs of his fingers. She feels the wedding band.

He kisses her again. And because the whole point of being with him is to make him happy, she gives up. "Can we turn off the light?" she asks.

Ron immediately switches off the overhead. There's still some light, though, coming from the parking lot. She sees the whites of Rob's eyes. She sees his silhouette, like any man's. He begins to undress her.

Under the covers she is able to stop worrying about Ron. For once, Rob is quiet. No laughing or fooling around. It seems possible that in the dark Ron won't realize what she and Rob are up to.

She is aware, obscurely, when there is bulk and movement on both sides of her. She is aware of skin pressed against her skin, back and front, of four hands on her.

But it takes a sound—a moan from one man and then from the other, as if an echo has passed through her—for her to get the picture.

"Oh, my God," she says.

They try to hold on to her. She punches at them and pulls free and runs to the bathroom.

"Hey, come on. What's the matter? Goddammit. Sandy!"

She locks the door. Shaking, crying, she sits on the toilet.

The door handle rattles. One of them—how is she supposed to know which one?—tells her to open up. "I want to talk to you," he says. She doesn't answer. "Baby?" It must be Rob. "What's the matter? Weren't we having a great time? Come on. There's nothing wrong if you're all having a great time."

"Go away!" she screams. She pulls off yards of toilet paper and weeps into it.

After a while she stops crying and looks at herself in the mirror above the sink. Nymphomaniac, she thinks leadenly. In the other room it is quiet. She lathers a washcloth and rubs at the streaks of mascara running down her face, wishing she'd grabbed her purse for the tube of cold cream she keeps in her makeup bag. She combs her hair with her fingers, wraps a towel around herself, and with the intention of getting dressed in silence and taking a taxi home, opens the door.

They are sitting side by side on the bed, drinking beer. All over again she is astonished at how alike they are. The same hunch of the shoulders, the same pot bellies. The same blue bikini underwear. The one closest to her stands and starts walking over.

"I'm not coming out," she says uncertainly, stepping back, glancing at his left hand and seeing the wedding band.

"Okay, I'll come in," he says. He closes the door, sits on the toilet and pulls her onto his lap.

"It's just so disgusting," she murmurs.

"Says who?"

"It just is."

"You were having a great time."

She pushes away from him. "No, I wasn't."

"Hey, I was there," he laughs, holding her tightly. "Listen, it's okay. There's nothing to be ashamed of. Everybody's into swinging. Movie stars have been into it for years. Frank Sinatra, Dean Martin and Natalie Wood? The three of them get it on together all the time."

"How do you know?"

"Everybody knows. It's in the papers."

She curls the grey hair behind his ear around her finger. She feels childish and on the verge of losing him.

"Ron thinks you're a knockout," he says.

She looks into his eyes. "Really?"

"Said you're the cutest thing he'd ever seen."

"Really?"

"Yeah. Sure."

She slumps against him. "Is there any sherry left?" she asks.

That night she keeps turning on the light, climbing out of bed and staring at herself in the dresser mirror. Over the next two days she feels like she's going to faint every time she thinks about what she has done and wants to do again. She looks up nymphomania in Lou's dictionary. "Excessive sexual desire by a female," it says. She looks up swinger. "A lively, up-to-date person."

On Wednesday night Rob is by himself. "Where's Ron?" she asks.

"Aren't I enough for you?" Rob laughs.

It turns out he isn't. When they're in bed, she feels a loss more overwhelming than the shame of feeling that loss, and she whispers, "I liked your brother."

On Sunday, there his brother is, in the passenger seat. He has another bottle of sherry. She finds that faced with both brothers, out of bed, she needs it. In bed, however, lying between them, she is transported. One ejaculates in her vagina, and the other in the crook of her neck. Then they all polish off the sherry and fall asleep. She dreams that their father smells the semen in her hair, knows it means she's a nymphomaniac and throws her down a snake pit. She wakes up in a sweat. And promptly falls back into a light sleep, in which she thinks she's at home, lying in bed between her sisters like the three of them used to do when they were little. A heavenly peace settles over her. Then she wakes up again, realizes where she actually is and bursts into tears.

The man on her left wakes up and says, "Oh, for Pete's sake."

The man on her rights says, "What's the matter?"

She tries to tell them part of it, about not being a nymphomaniac after all, but they don't understand what she's talking about, so she gives up. With relief and for old times, and after a few minutes for everything that feels like a loss—Rapunzel, Jimmy, the Santa Claus man, their mother's hair before it went white—she cries her heart out.

At the top of the street Lou has let the baby carriage go. She always does; it's not much of a hill. But this time the carriage has raced too far ahead of her. And a car is coming.

"Stop!" she screams. She runs as hard as she can. She waves her arms. She can't believe that the driver doesn't see her or the carriage. The carriage is speeding up, heading for the intersection. Heading straight and stupid as an arrow.

Lou knows that the carriage and the car will reach the middle of the intersection at exactly the same instant. She screams. The car screams, braking. It hits the carriage, sends it flying. The baby pops out and lands near the curb.

Lou falls beside him. He's on his back, crying. His face is as red as blood but not bleeding. She pulls off his hood and wool toque.

The driver comes rushing over. "Is it all right?" he says. He kneels down. "Jesus Christ, I didn't even see you."

You? Does he think that Lou was holding onto the carriage? She glances at him. A guy their father's age. "You should watch where you're going," she says angrily.

"I know," he says. "I'm sorry. God."

A red bump is on the back of the baby's head. "Good Lord," the man says, then stands and hurries off.

"It's okay, honey, it's okay," Lou says to the baby. She touches the bump. He cries louder. Gently she lifts him and rests him against her legs so that she can take off his jacket.

The man returns. "Wrap it in this," he says, holding out a trench coat. "I'll drive it to the hospital."

"He's okay," she says. But she snatches the coat and folds it up to lay the baby on. Now she can pull his pants off.

"That bump looks bad," the man says.

"It's not soft," Lou says. She's got some idea that soft means internal bleeding.

More people are around now. A couple of kids and a woman wearing red-checkered oven mitts. "They came out of nowhere," the man says to the woman.

"Should I call an ambulance?" the woman asks.

"No!" Lou snaps. In a calmer voice she adds, "It's only a bump."

"Why are you taking all his clothes off?" the woman asks.

Because she is searching for another wound. The fatal one. She realizes she's gone too far, removing his socks and diaper. "I've got to wrap him in this coat," she answers firmly, as if it's obvious he needs to be undressed for that. Although she takes care not to touch the back of his head, he struggles and begins to cry in long, shivery squeals. The weirdest sound. Lou feels like laughing. Pressing him to her chest, pressing where laughter will erupt from, she comes to her feet and orders one of the kids to pick up his clothes.

The man has turned the carriage upright. A wheel is bent. "I can put this in the trunk and drive you both to the hospital," the man says, sounding a little reluctant, sounding worried now that she'll say okay. Well, she's way ahead of him. The minute he mentioned the word *hospital,* she saw some smart doctor, a Dr. Kildare type, bringing in the police.

"You better have him checked out just in case," the woman says.

"I will," Lou lies. "My father can drive him." The little boy she told to pick up the clothes hands them to her, looking extremely concerned. "I once caught a bullfrog for fishing," he confides. "And when I put the hook in it, it cried just like that."

Before they reach his house, the baby stops crying. Inside, on the front hall floor, Lou unwraps the trench coat to check him for injuries again. Other than the bump, there is nothing. This strikes her as miraculous. The bump is huge and purple now, but she can touch it now without him squawking. She gets his bottle and moves it around in front of his face. His eyes follow it like radar, and since this is the only sign of intelligence she's ever witnessed in him, she decides he hasn't suffered brain damage.

Her story will be that she was out walking him when she slipped on a patch of ice and pulled over the carriage as she fell. She'll say that she should never have been asked to walk him in the first place, in these treacherous conditions. She'll ask for an hourly raise. She'll tie some gauze around her wrist.

He cries when she leaves him to heat his milk but stops on a dime when she puts the bottle in his hands. Wrapping him back up, she wonders where she can unload the trench coat for a few bucks. She carries him into the living room, sits on the chesterfield and starts to cry.

Until he's finished the bottle, she cries and tells him she's sorry. She wants to mean it. She wants to love him. She wants to love him and for him to know that she loves him. He's just a little baby, she tells herself. But all she can feel is how heavy he is in her arms.

On the way there Norma pulls the car over three times to wipe fog from the windshield and from her glasses. When she finally figures out that the heater is sending out blasts of cold steam, she tries to turn it off. Their father won't let her. He will never admit that anything is the matter with his car.

She's only wearing a thin spring jacket. That's what he tossed at her on the way out the door. He made her hurry, as if they were late for an important appointment. As if this parking spot on a dirt road in the middle of nowhere would be taken.

She's tired of these drives. Fed up, and that's the truth. Keeping him company, thinking pure thoughts, praying and praying for him . . . none of it's doing him any good. In fact, he seems more depressed than ever. As for learning how to drive, she's sure she could have sailed through her test a month ago, but he won't let her take the car to an exam center. It's nuts. What do you expect from a psychotic alcoholic? Lou asks.

Norma glances over at him. He's staring at her arm with that sleepy expression he gets by the end of the six pack. But she thinks he's had more than six, she thinks he was drinking at home before they left. She leans against the steering wheel and wipes the windshield. Black clouds tumble up from the horizon, just as if a line of fires burns there. It makes her uncomfortable how his eyes fall on her after he's been drinking. At least it means they can leave soon, though.

"Looks like a snowstorm's coming," she says so that he'll say, "Let's go."

"Are you cold?" he asks in a sudden way.

"Yeah, freezing."

He holds up a finger to wait and opens his door. Skidding on the ice, banging the hood for support, he makes it to the trunk and is a long time searching his pockets for his extra set of keys. She knows that he's getting the blanket and that saying she doesn't need it is useless. She is about to give him the keys in the ignition, when she hears his set drop on the ground and in a few seconds drop again. The simplest thing would be for her to open the trunk herself, but she can't imagine taking over from him like that. She thinks of something else Lou said. The other night. They were in the kitchen, and their mother was calling from the TV room for some more "coffee," and Lou, taking the whiskey bottle out of the cupboard, said, "Considering our upbringing, it's amazing one of us is normal." There was no question she was referring to herself.

Their father opens the passenger door. His face is triumphant. "This'll warm you up," he says thickly, climbing in.

She sighs.

"Shhh," he says.

He tosses the blanket over her legs and smooths it out.

She stiffens. And is instantly worried about offending him. But he goes on smoothing, very slowly and intently and ineffectively. His thoughts seem to have drifted. She looks out her window.

When his hand slips under the blanket, he continues to make smoothing motions, as though he doesn't realize where he's strayed. His breathing quivers. She has stopped breathing.

He smooths her leg. Up her legs, up to her stomach.

Under her sweater.

She lets out her breath.

His hand is ice.

His head drops to her breasts.

"Don't," she whispers.

His hand roves all over her.

"Please," she whispers. "Dad."

His surprised, waking-up face lifts. She smells his beer breath. She shoves him away, and he flops back against his door.

She opens her door, climbs out. The blanket is wrapped around her left leg, and it hangs on as she runs. She can't kick it off. She has to yank it free with both hands.

At the end of the road she stops running and looks back. The blanket, halfway between her and the car, has an animal's shape. Something run-over. The car leans into the ditch. There is the blanket and the car and the fields.

Her heart beats in her ears, clangs like bells. Where their father touched her, she burns. She thinks that she must tear off her jacket and sweater and lie her flaming skin on the frozen ground. She covers her face with her hands and is lost for several minutes in a dark profoundness of disgust and incomprehension.

"Jimmy," she says into her hands.

What is their father doing? Crying. She has an image in her mind of him crying, of his remorse. She feels a pang and feels it blow out like a match in this wind. Then she feels the cold. She walks back to the car and sees the suggestion of him through the fogged-up glass. He appears to be smoking.

After she opens the door, she stands there for a minute. His hand draws out the ashtray and extinguishes his cigarette. By the time she gets in, he is turned away, resting his head on his arm. She doesn't believe he is asleep.

She switches off the heater and drives away without wiping the windshield. Guessing where the road is.

DANCE TO THE MUSIC

1968

The next morning Norma looks back at who she's been and winces at her prayers and her appeals to their dead brother. No wonder Lou makes fun of her.

She feels rescued by the person she used to be, a person that for a long time has been waiting in the wings. Driving home from the country, she glanced at herself in the rearview mirror and saw strength. Not divine or physical strength. But her old common sense. And something more—a toughness. She knew two things for certain then. One was that she wasn't their mother, she wasn't going to cave in and have Lou and Sandy take over. The other was that her new strength would scald his hand.

She keeps him out of her line of vision. He's a shadow with a foot that drags. To his face Lou accuses him of playing up his limp for sympathy.

"I may lose the leg," he replies with dignity.

Norma deflects that plea. Since she doesn't think of him, she doesn't think of forgiving him.

She gets her driver's license, cuts her hair short and gives Sandy the red angora sweater again. She goes off her diet and gains twenty-five pounds in two months.

Her friends praise her for not trying to be somebody she isn't. But they fret over her independence, calling it dangerous, whereas when she was slimmer, they called it snobbery.

"We've got to stick together," they warn her. They say, "What did we tell you?" when she walks down the halls by herself and is mooed at.

"It doesn't bother me," Norma says truthfully. All her former fears are gone. She undresses for Phys. Ed. with the other girls in her class and doesn't care if they gawk. She writes her exams as coolly as if she were in a room by herself. She applies for and gets a summer job at the hardware store and is commended by the owner for her know-how and unflappability. On Sunday she cleans the house. In the evenings she walks to the ravine and waits under the trestle bridge for trains to pass over.

The basement is only half finished, but she doesn't work on it. Except to do the laundry, she doesn't go down there anymore. Their father doesn't go down the basement, either. He's stopped drinking, so he doesn't make trips down to the fridge. He couldn't manage the stairs anyway, on account of his bad foot.

In July he goes into the hospital, to have his leg amputated, he announces, but it's only to have his foot put back together the way it should have been when he shot it years ago.

The operation is a failure, and the instant he learns this, his fury returns. While still in the hospital, he takes out a lawsuit against the place and against the doctors who did the bad job to begin with. He writes letters to the daily papers, calling for a government inquiry. "Give him a lobotomy," is Lou's advice to his doctor. What the doctors give him is a big check, settling the matter out of court. With part of the money he buys a new car from where he works. A white Oldsmobile. "A whore lure," Lou calls it, although he doesn't seem to be pining for a Lovergirl. He's his old self—foul-tempered, laying down the law. But he doesn't hit Lou or Norma, even at the peak of his most lunatic rages. It seems he's gone off hitting.

Lou doesn't believe the restraint will last. But it better, for his sake. After the last time he backhanded her, that day he took Norma out for her first driving lesson, she told herself she'd kill him if he ever laid a finger on her again. When he was in the hospital, she went down to the bomb shelter, took his World War II gun off the wall and pointed it at where his head would be if he were sleeping on his bunk. She couldn't actually imagine pulling the trigger, but it felt like a step forward that she at least had the nerve to aim.

Now that he's out of the hospital, bawling her out every time he lays eyes on her, she thinks of aiming his gun and doesn't lose control. Sometimes she ignores him, and that really drives him up the wall. She walks a fine line between insolence and the showdown.

With her sisters it's another story. One day, partly to explain her behavior since birth, partly to get the three of them talking again, she says, "This house is like a dangerous country that is ruled by a despot and founded on an historical calamity."

The calamity is their mother, if Norma and Sandy care to ask. They don't. Oh, Lou knows why not. All the abuse she's handed out, especially to Norma. She's not so bad these days, though. She controls herself. She keeps thinking that nobody loves her, and it worries her that she's even concerned enough to have the thought. She helps Norma with the dishes, but Norma doesn't exactly fall on her knees with gratitude. In fact, Norma doesn't seem to realize that the last time Lou picked up a dishtowel was a year ago. Lou used to find Norma as easy to read and confide in as a diary. Now Norma, and Sandy, too, are both closed books. Or foreign books. Untranslatable.

Their father obviously finds their isolation threatening. At supper time he actually tries to stir up arguments between them: "Lou, if what Sandy just said bothers you, say so. Speak freely." In his better moods he start up singsongs and suggests family projects, such as collecting bottles for the church. "Where's your get up and go?" he bellows. Lou smirks at her sisters, who don't look at her. Even in dashing their father's hopes, there's no confederacy. Eventually, Lou loses heart. "Fuck them," she tells herself with less conviction than she'd like. She begins to wish for a boyfriend. Someone to be madly in love with.

Sandy doesn't miss Rob. Or his twin brother. Or any older men. She is afraid that after a few weeks she'll start to, that she has an addiction. But while she sometimes aches with an indefinite longing, she has no longing for the old remedy. She is too aware now of the reasons why it isn't a good idea: all the lying and sneaking around; the tightrope walking; their father's sarcastic "Off to some sleazy motel?" because of her short skirts, because he has no idea that she's really off to some sleazy motel; her friends' suspicion about why she never goes out on dates anymore. One of her friends says, "I thought I should tell you. A rumor's going around that you've turned into a lesbian." Horrified, Sandy phones a guy she's been out with a few times, a giant he-man, and asks him to take her bowling.

After she breaks up with Rob, she starts dating this guy regularly. His name is Dave. He's two years older than her and twice as tall. A football player who failed grade nine or ten.

Anything you plug in, he knows how to fix. At his father's appliance store, where he works after school, he's the service department. Just like Sandy, he shines in a store, and when she learns this about him, she lets him undo her bra.

"Thanks," he says.

She's led him to believe that no guy has every touched her bare breasts. "She's not a lesbian, but she's not a slut," is the message she intends for him to broadcast. But as his huge hand cups her breast with devout gentleness, she realizes that this will be his message even if she sleeps with him.

Still, when he asks a few days later if he can please feel her "down there," she says no.

"Okay," he says. Polite, no hard feelings. She knows that she can't hold him off forever, but she likes this new sensation of feeling loved without making love.

Dave insists on picking Sandy up at her house. He says it doesn't sit right with him, parking down the street, or meeting in a restaurant (her next suggestion). "I know about your mother's drinking problem," he offers gallantly.

Maybe. But he doesn't know about their father. For several months, on the evenings she and Dave have a date, she waits in the front hall and runs out as soon as his car pulls up in the driveway. Then one night he shows up half an hour early, while she's still in her bedroom getting dressed, and before she can do anything about it, their father answers the door.

"What is it?" he asks threateningly.

"Good evening, sir," Dave says. "I'm here for Sandy."

"I see!" their father shouts.

Silence. Sandy pictures their father's speechless surprise. All her life she has discouraged friends, girls and boys, from calling on her. It's her surest instinct. She opens her bedroom door, about to call "I'll meet you in the car!" when their father shouts, "Come in!"

"Thank you," Dave says. "I'm afraid I'm early. Sorry about that."

"I didn't catch the name!" their father says, still shouting.

Dave shouts his name, bellows it, and Sandy thinks, "Oh, my God," but their father only shouts, "We have a Dave at work." Sandy shuts her door and start tearing the rollers out of her hair.

When she comes running down the hall, their father looks relieved and still surprised. "All set?" he shouts.

She sits on the bench to pull on her boots. There across from her is the hole in the wall where years ago their father hurled the vacuum cleaner right through. What will she tell Dave caused it? Their father trims the lawn with scissors, but he hasn't fixed that hole yet.

"Okay," she says, standing. "Bye."

Their father slaps Dave on the shoulder. "Have fun at the orgy!" he says. Dave laughs.

"Stay away from the dope fiends!" their father jokes.

Sandy laughs at this one. She can't believe how nice their father is being. Maybe it's because Dave also has a brush cut. She gives their father a look. She thinks, this is how he must have been—funny, friendly—when their mother met him, during the war.

Lou dreams she is standing at the edge of what somebody has informed her are the White Cliffs of Dover. She is with a boy who has an English accent and rings on every finger. It's a half sleeping, half waking dream. The rings are how she knows she's drifted off. She supposes that the boy is Tom and that she's mixed him up with Ringo Starr instead of with John Lennon.

Tom is the new boy at school. Tom Fenton. Thomas. T.F. Tom and Lou. T.F. and L.F. Lou writes variations everywhere, on all her notebooks, on the soles of her running shoes, backwards on her eraser to make a stamp. On her wrist with a needle: T.F. in dots of blood, and one night, in a frenzy of ardor, a *T,* on her stomach in two razor lines. Of all the girls who think they love him, she believes that she is the only one who sees beyond his John Lennon face, wire-rimmed glasses and British accent. What she sees, what thrills her, is the cold look in his eye. She has that look, too, she thinks.

He's in her English class. He calls Robert Frost, whom the teacher reveres, a third-rate poet. He says that "Acquainted with the Night" is not about man's inhumanity to man but about the void in man. In the corridors he strides alone and scowling, usually reading a library book.

"Ten bucks says he's a homo," is Sherry's reaction when Lou tells her he hasn't asked any girl out. Sherry has quit school, lied about her age and gotten a job as a cocktail waitress at The Nineteenth Hole, the golf-and-country-club restaurant. Sherry says that English guys are either completely homo or half and half. "Take it from me," she says.

For once Lou doesn't want to hear the sordid proof. "Not Tom," she says. She has the idea that homosexuals are flamboyant and happy. Also rare.

Sherry makes a circle with her thumb and forefinger and pokes her other forefinger in and out. "There's only one way to know for sure," she says.

"Give me time," Lou says.

She tries to impress him by faking his interests. All the advice (she lowers herself to seeking it in Sandy's fashion magazines, and she's influenced by what Jean Peters did to catch Louis Jourdan in *Three Coins in the Fountain*) seems to boil down to Fake His Interests. She takes out of the library the books she sees him carrying: *Siddhartha, The Fountainhead, The Collected Poems of Wallace Stevens.* She reads them walking. She buys wire-rimmed glasses. After seeing him smoking a cigarette on his way home from school, she smokes right out in the corridors.

She clings to two straws. One, that he doesn't seem to be noticing any of her competitors either. Two, that none of her competitors is as smart and reckless as she is. She will do anything to win him. Anything.

Stella for star, as everyone who as seen *A Streetcar Named Desire* (and Norma has seen it three times) knows.

Did Stella's parents name her after the girl in the movie, or was she born dazzling? Norma wonders and daydreams. Stella is her dream girl. Probably she's the dream girl of half the boys at school, too, but no boy has the nerve to ask her out. Stella is over six feet tall and has white-blonde waistlong hair and a face as sweet as a baby's. You can understand why her parents didn't press their luck. (Stella is an only child.) Her parents adore her. They take her to the Caribbean on holidays. Everything there is to know about Stella from a distance, Norma knows.

The first day after the Thanksgiving holiday Norma manages to stand behind Stella in the cafeteria line. This is all the heaven Norma feels she wants and deserves. Although she daydreams, she never hopes.

Stella has been away for a week, to Jamaica, and she has a bad sunburn. Her long hand reaching for a carton of milk is blistered, and when Norma sees this, she gasps, which makes Stella turn around and look at her.

Norma feels herself blush. She hasn't blushed in months; she thought she'd outgrown it. "You should put calamine lotion on your hand," she murmurs.

"Pardon me?" Stella says. She tosses her hair back.

"Calamine lotion."

Stella waits.

"It takes away the burn and stops some of the peeling," Norma says. She shrugs, mortified now. "It's just a suggestion."

But Stella is supremely interested. Inclining her head, she asks if you can buy calamine lotion without a prescription. She asks how much it costs. Then she says, "Gee, thanks a lot," and offers Norma such a sweet, gorgeous smile that Norma feels an old stirring of sadness connected with her desire to serve a paragon, and she offers to bring Stella a bottle of calamine lotion from home.

"Oh, no," Stella says. "I mean, thanks anyway, but I wouldn't want to use all yours up." Her slender, burned hand taps Norma's. "I know," she says. "Why don't we walk home together and go to the drugstore on the way?"

They become best friends. It's the most amazing thing that has ever happened to Norma. At the end of classes, there is this glorious girl waiting at her locker, looking around anxiously as if Norma might go home without her. As if!

Stella's nature and coloring and beauty remind Norma of Sandy. "I love you *so* much," Sandy used to say. "I think you're *so* great," Stella says when Norma figures out some math problem, when she throws the discus farther than anyone else in gym class. Stella feels the muscles in Norma's arm and squeals with admiration. Shrugging off her own breathtaking hair as tangly and always in the way, she says that Norma's hair is practical and that she wishes her mother would allow her to get the same cut.

"Don't you dare!" Norma says.

When she and Stella walk together, Stella sometimes holds her hand.

At the beginning of the second feature, in the front seat of Dave's father's car (the back seat being filled with boxes of Waring blenders), Sandy and Dave go all the way.

Sandy squeezes her vagina tight (Dave isn't as big as she expected from how tall he is) and makes noises of pain. "Sorry," he says. "Sorry. Sorry." She watches the movie. It's about a monster baby that preys on milkmen.

In the few moments it takes for the baby to be born and to escape out of an air vent, Dave has entered her and come. The car is washed in screen light (the baby emerging into the day) just as he opens his eyes. He gazes down at her with such thankfulness that she's tempted to own up then and there.

But she doesn't. Feeling herself drip onto the seat, she reaches for the pile of napkins. They've arrived prepared. The big night has been planned to coincide with their three-month anniversary of going out together. Also with the first day of her period, although Dave doesn't know this part.

"That's life," has been Dave's summing up of all her secrets, including Niagara Falls. She bets she could tell him she went around shooting people, and he'd wrap his eighteen-inch-bicep arm around her and say it was life. But she can't see him calling her affairs with balding, married men whose names begin with *R* life. His secret is that he fainted once, giving blood, and she imagines a crash like a falling tree. Anyway, she asks herself, why hurt him sooner than she has to?

He assumes they're going to be married. He has it arranged that after graduation they'll live in the apartment above the appliance store, him working in the service department, and her working as a cashier until she gets pregnant. He assumes this despite knowing about her ambition to leave school at the end of the year and use the money she's saved to go to college and study fashion design. Despite having seen some of the drawings she intends to send in with her application. Either he thinks that the college won't accept her or that she won't go when it comes down to it. Or maybe he really doesn't understand what her being accepted will mean. "We'll save money with you sewing your own clothes" is all he says when she shows him the drawings. She decides then not to straighten him out. Soon enough she'll be breaking his heart. Whether she's accepted or not, she can't marry somebody she doesn't love. In the meantime the least she can do for a boy who loves her enough to want to live with her for the rest of his life (no married man wanted that) is to let him go all the way.

"Look at all the blood," he says, holding the napkins up to the light. He sounds both worried and gratified.

Sandy is watching the movie. A slow close-up is in progress, the first sight of the baby. From a distance the baby seems cute. Then, as you get nearer, you see that it has deranged eyes. The camera travels right into its howling mouth, to its tonsils and down a black and red tunnel—the route that the swallowed milkmen take.

Dave turns his attention back to the screen. "The birth canal," he says authoritatively.

Sandy bursts out laughing.

"What?" he says. She shakes her head, unable to speak. "C'mon," he laughs, "what's so funny?"

She can't tell him. She's laughing too hard, and, besides, she doesn't know what's *so* funny. She points to the screen, where in a few minutes he'll figure out his mistake.

The vice-principal catches Lou smoking in the corridors and threatens her with suspension. Later that day, in English class, Tom says that Charlotte Corday was a saint, so the next day Lou brings in a bread knife and lets it be known she intends to use it if the vice-principal threatens her again. Feeling a terrifying exhilaration, she rises to a dare and smokes a cigarette right outside the closed door of the vice-principal's office.

She doesn't see Tom come up behind her. When his hand reaches around and snatches the cigarette out of her mouth, she thinks he's the vice-principal. "It's not worth it," he says.

She is speechless.

He takes a puff of her cigarette. "If you have to do somebody in," he says, "go to Washington. Pick off Nixon." He drops the cigarette to the floor and extinguishes it under the high heel of his brown suede boot. "Get into heaven."

"No chance," she says, meaning about heaven. Her laugh is shrill, crazy-sounding. "Anyway," she says, infuriated by the laugh, "I need some target practice first," and she draws the knife out of her purse and stabs it into the wood alongside the vice-principal's door. She stares at it, awed.

Tom grabs her arm. "Let's go," he says quietly. He pulls her down the hall, running with her to the side exit. Still holding her arm, although she isn't resisting, he leads her through the parking lot to a beat-up red Volkswagen in the corner. He opens the passenger door. "Climb in," he says, then strides around, opens the driver's door, throws his books on the back seat and gets in.

"Is this yours?" she asks, surprised.

"No." He glowers, pushing in the lighter.

"Whose is it?"

"I don't know. It was unlocked."

"Ha!" she says happily. She kicks off her shoes and puts her feet up on the dash. Her skirt rises up her bare thighs. She feels more relief that she shaved her legs last night than that she didn't have to stab the vice-principal.

Tom lights a cigarette from the lighter and another from the lit cigarette. She wants him to direct hers between her lips but isn't disappointed by the way he hands it over without glancing at her, as if they do this all the time.

As the keys have been left in the ignition, she suggests stealing the car, stopping off at her house for their father's gun and driving to

Washington. He calls her a weird bird. She detects admiration in his voice. "You should meet my mother," she says, her greatest extravagance so far.

He turns on the engine but only for the heater, not to drive anywhere. He goes back to talking about Nixon. Nixon could end the Vietnam War tomorrow, he says, but doesn't want to because of his Mafia mentality. He calls Nixon a fucking asshole. He sucks on his cigarette, looking murderous with rage, and she is dizzy with love. All her rage is personal, directed against their father and her own unjust circumstances. She decides that from now on she'll be angry about Nixon and Vietnam. About war. "There never was a good war," Tom says. "Benjamin Franklin."

She luxuriates in being able to look at him up close as he looks out the window. She studies his right ear that is pointed like an elf's, his sideburn that has red hair in it, his noble nose. She accepts all she sees as the highest standard. At the same time she ransacks her brain for war facts and remembers the first two lines of a poem they studied last year in English—Wilfred Owen's "Arms and the Boy." She recites:

Let the boy try along this bayonet blade
How cold steel is, and keen with hunger of blood.

But most of her attention is devoted to wondering if Tom will touch her, kiss her. Ask her out.

When the three-fifteen bell rings and they have to leave the car, Tom says offhandedly, "Why don't you pop round to my house this evening? The old man and lady are out. We'll have the place to ourselves."

She hurries home. On the way she sees a one-armed man walking a lame dog. It's the dog she feels sorry for. She suspects the man of having kicked it lame. Because the man is missing an arm, she assumes he's developed a twisted personality. Tom, she thinks, is perfect, and therefore she trusts him, not to be kind, that's for sure, but to be much more than that, much better: to be intelligent, to have elevated scope.

She has a bath and shaves her legs again. Then she has a shower and washes her hair and fills the tub and has another bath in Sandy's jasmine-scented oil, which she didn't notice before. Then she washes her hair again in water that has gone cold.

She can't tell if she is happy and terrified or just terrified. Extreme happiness and terror have always felt the same to her. She knows she is making herself very clean as some meager compensation for her complete sexual inexperience. Until today being a virgin has been a vague affliction. Now it is the excruciating crux of her life. For all the porn she's read and all that Sherry has told her, she doesn't even know how to kiss.

What does Tom expect of her? She is frantic that she's misled him with her slutty vocabulary and the bread knife. She tries to picture his face so that she can examine it for signs of intent, but she can only conjure up Lennon's face from her *Revolver* album.

But it's *him* she loves. Tom. To confirm it she looks down at the scab of the cross she cut on her stomach with the razor. If he acts like he loves her, she'll tell him what the cross stands for.

Barely looking at her, Tom mumbles, "You're here" and strides away. Lou follows him down the hall, through the kitchen and down the basement stairs.

The only thing she spots looking like it's from England is a pair of crossed swords displayed above the stairwell. When she touches them, they turn out to be plastic. She could be in a version of her own house except for the smell that's often in other people's places, a rotting smell, which she used to think was the odor of a normal household but which she now recognizes as the odor of cooked meat. In their house, except for hot dogs, they eat meat already cooked in the can.

At the bottom of the stairs Tom stops, extracts a key from his pants pocket and opens a door. She is reminded of Lance Nipper opening the door to the apartment-building laundry room, of the nail tearing her insides, and she shivers and is incredulous to think of her small young self so violated. Collusion, she thinks, is the difference between that time and this. She asks Tom why the door is locked. "Privacy," he answers. He lights a match.

She sees the bed first. He is walking around lighting candles. They are in Coke and beer bottles on the desk and bookcase and window ledge. Candlelight is bomb-shelter light to her. It makes her claustrophobic. Tom squats in front of the bookcase and starts filing through the records on the bottom shelf. "Sit down, why don't you?" he says.

There is only the bed. She takes her jacket off first, dropping it on the floor in an act of casualness. She sits on the end of the bed farthest from him and leans back against the wood-panelled wall, her legs in their skin-tight jeans (at the last minute she had Sandy take the jeans in) striking her as inhumanly long and thin. Will they turn him off? Who gives a shit, she thinks. She's been feeling this way since she arrived, and she wonders if it's typically virginal or only typical of her, or if she really has some sensible reason for wanting to back out. Right at this moment she couldn't say she loves him.

He puts on a record, stands and turns to face her, leaning against the bookcase. It's a Bob Dylan record—she recognizes the voice, not the song. "I wish he'd blow his nose," she says.

"Listen," Tom growls.

Her heart jumps. The candles flame up. Tom just stands there, arms folded, frowning into the space between them, all during that song and most of the next. Finally he speaks, says, "Dylan is one of the few intelligent lyricists at work today," then lights two cigarettes and hands one to her, and they start talking about songwriters. She praises Lennon and mentions the physical resemblance. "I don't see it," Tom says dismissively. He approves of Lennon, though—"a naive genius." He proceeds to deliver a lecture about genius. He paces, spanning the room in three long strides, he sprawls on the other end of the bed, gets up, turns the record over, paces. Vigilant and reconciled and sweating from a mild fit of claustrophobia, she waits for him to make a pass. She notices a little pipe, like a bubble-blowing pipe, on the dresser, and presently she goes over and picks it up.

For the first time since she's arrived, he looks right at her. "Do you want to smoke some grass?" he asks.

"Sure," she says, as if she has before.

Tom pushes up the window an inch. The cold draft blows out the candles on the ledge. He sits beside her on the bed, and their upper arms touch. She looks at him. In the cruel squint of his eye as he lights the pipe, she sees everything she wants. Now she could say she loves him. She is careful to do what he does. Inhale hard, hold in the smoke. She coughs, and he slaps her back.

Being so close to him, putting her lips where his lips have just been, breaking the law with him, feeling love and not feeling whatever it is—a blockage, a brick wall, a suspicion—that before has always alchemized love into something else (usually anger) make this moment the most exquisite in her life so far. She goes into a trance of love. She lies against the pillows.

He gets up to put on another Bob Dylan record. He stays over at the bookcase and starts talking about Sigmund Freud, about women carrying purses because they have wombs. The candle flames thrash. He speaks in tongues. Her lungs shrink to the size of raisins, and not even the river of icy air streaming from the window to her mouth can inflate them. "You're stoned," she thinks to reassure herself. Untold minutes pass. She tries to retrace a mesh of thought back to its source, but the end of the thought, which is that he's not going to fuck her tonight or even kiss her, keeps interfering with her concentration.

When they hear the front door open, he throws the bag of grass and the pipe behind some books and shuts the window. Blows out the candles, switches on the blinding overhead light. It's like the end of a movie.

"Let's go," he says.

Up in the kitchen are two small terrified-looking people, still in hats. "Mum, Dad—Lou Field," Tom mutters, walking right by them.

They smile anxiously at Lou, the father glancing at her tight jeans. "Don't shit yourself," Lou wants to say, "nothing happened." In the front hall she puts on her jacket in silence. Tom opens the door for her.

"Bye," she says indifferently, expecting the same from him.

But he says, "See you at school tomorrow," in a conspiratorial voice, and she feels his fingers brush the ends of her hair.

Sleep is out of the question. She turns on her flashlight and starts reading the Wallace Stevens book she borrowed from the library a couple of days ago. She commits three poems to memory. The next day at lunch Tom sits at her table, and they eat together. Her competitors all look suicidal. Ten years later the recollection of their devastation will still lift her spirits. She directs the conversation to Wallace

Stevens, specifically to the three memorized poems: "Domination of Black," "The Paltry Nude Starts on a Spring Voyage" and "Girl in a Nightgown," pretending to summon them back after a long time. She chose them for their sexy titles and reasonably short lengths, but he broods about what her attachment to their themes means.

"Peacocks, Aphrodite and sensual awakening," he says. "What unites all three? What would Freud say?"

By the end of the day the rumor is they're going steady. She doesn't deny it. Maybe he hears it and is influenced, because he starts eating with her every lunch hour. Some days he waits for her at her locker, and they walk home together. They smoke grass in anyone's unlocked car and once a week in his basement bedroom when his parents go to an English pub downtown.

All they do is talk about what they've read. To keep up with him, she has to read library books until two or three o'clock in the morning. She is tired all the time. Not just from late nights but from acting the way she thinks he wants her to, which is deadly serious and angry about world events. She tells Sherry that they're sleeping together, but after a month he hasn't even kissed her on the lips. Saying goodbye he sometimes pecks her on the cheek, and once, sharing her umbrella, he put his arm around her. Obviously he likes her (she's the only person he hangs around with) but she can't tell if he's in love with her. Maybe he's just taking it slow. Maybe there are English courtship rules she doesn't know about.

Maybe it's her. That idea begins to incense her, because she knows she turns men on. When she wears Sandy's miniskirts, workmen whistle at her. "Jesus fucking Christ, what does he want?" she shouts at her mirror, all terror concerning sexual inexperience long ago jettisoned.

In daydreams she makes the first move. There are so many opportunities to kiss him. What stops her more than fear of being rejected (she has imagined all the humiliating variations, as well as her subsequent vengeance) is fear of having nobody to love.

"I'm in heaven," Norma thinks when she is with Stella. Sometimes she thinks that Stella is an angel. The evidence is strong, and although Norma doesn't pray anymore, she still believes in God and the possibility of miracles.

Stella is so lovely, so perfect. Her angel's hair shimmers down her back, her skin is milky and flawless, her teeth white and straight. She smells of baby powder. And an angel *would* be tall, Norma reasons. An embodiment of glory would, more than likely, be tall.

Stella says (having never been given reason to think otherwise), "People are good underneath." Her parents call her Bunny. Every time she enters a room that they're in, they exclaim; they get up and give her a hug and a kiss. They are medium-sized brown-haired people who can't seem to get over the daughter they've made.

When Stella was five years old, her favorite uncle died. Her parents hid their grief and told her that the uncle had gone on a world tour. They even arranged to have postcards sent to the house from foreign lands. This went on for five years, until one day Stella happened to say that she barely remembered Uncle So-and-so, and only then did her parents break the news.

They tell her that fish don't feel the hook. They rave over her C-average report card, claiming that girls who get high marks are unfeminine.

"Right, Norma?" they ask.

"Yeah, right," Norma says. No more than they does she want the truth to tarnish this precious girl.

Before Norma knew to be careful, she mentioned that their father used to hit her. She didn't think it was any big deal. But Stella was horrified, then inconsolable. She actually burst into tears, and to stop her crying, Norma had to swear that she was just kidding, that their father wouldn't hurt a flea. She'd have sworn to anything. They were sitting on Stella's bed, and as Norma fabricated a golden childhood, she held Stella tightly in her arms.

Twenty times a day Norma relives this moment. It has crossed her mind to let slip another old hardship so that Stella will fall shuddering against her. But Norma shudders at such a mean thought.

All the things Stella likes to do—read fashion magazines, practice putting on makeup, curl her hair in juice cans, talk about what's going on at school—are harmless, girlish things. They are things a saint wouldn't see fit to do, Norma grants that, but an angel, containing no evil or earthly know-how, might fall into them. Anyway, watching Stella do them is Norma's definition of heaven on earth. It's like watching a beloved baby at play. In Stella's company the only time Norma is unhappy is when she gets a weird feeling that Stella is Sandy, and then she thinks how Sandy has turned into the kind of girl who wears short skirts and tight sweaters and necks with boys. Whenever Norma thinks this, she becomes her old self, assuming all blame for everything—Sandy's decline, everything. The feeling doesn't last long. A few minutes or so. She gets over it.

Tom calculates that if they drop a half a tab in fifteen minutes, they'll be tripping by New Year's.

It's quarter to eleven. Tom is lying on his bed, Lou is standing at his dresser. All the candles are lit, and Jefferson Airplane is on the record player. Tom's parents are out at the English pub.

"A *half?*" Lou says, pressing her finger to one of the tabs of LSD and picking it up. It's like a square sequin but even thinner than that. She can't believe a half will be enough, because these days it takes a lot of grass to get her stoned. "You're talking to the daughter of a woman whose tolerance of intoxicants is immeasurable," she says.

"A whole tab will blow your mind straight through the roof," Tom says. She flicks the tab off her thumb, back onto the piece of foil with the other one. She says she's game.

She's not trying to impress him. She has resolved that tonight is her last night as a virgin, and she is relying on this acid trip to compel her to take her clothes off. If he isn't turned on by her naked, at least she'll be able to deny she had intentions. In *Time* magazine she read that people on LSD are overcome with a desire to undress and jump out of windows. When she told this to Tom, he said, "We'll be in the basement." She'd like to think he's staging tonight to get her nude, but she doubts it. He'd have kissed her before now, tested the waters.

"I'm serious," she says. "Let's drop a whole tab each."

In the mirror Tom gives her a condescending smile. "Check with me at midnight," he says. "If you want more then, I won't stand in your way."

When fifteen minutes are up, they swallow the LSD with beer, then lie on the bed and wait. Propped up on one elbow, Tom reads from his current passion, *The Tibetan Book of the Dead:* "There is no need to fear. The lords of death are the natural form of emptiness, your own confused projection, and you are emptiness. . . ."

After about twenty minutes he closes the book and takes off his glasses. She doesn't wear glasses anymore. A couple of weeks ago she broke the pair she bought, and since she was starting to get afraid anyway that he would discover the lenses were just ordinary glass, she didn't bother to buy another pair. She's never seen him without his glasses. His eyes are green, long-lashed and inscrutable.

"What happens first?" she asks.

"It depends." He stretches out beside her and folds his arms behind his head. It's all she can do not to roll over and lie against him. It's all she can do.

"Why?" he asks after a minute. "Is something happening?"

"No, I don't think so."

"You'll *know* so." He's told her that this is his third acid trip.

The record ends, and he puts on Jimi Hendrix. Over the music she can hear her heartbeat. It's the most desolate sound she can imagine. Her eyes fill with tears. And then she begins slowly to levitate, and simultaneously lights burst in her head, and she is ecstatic. The whole of *The Tibetan Book of the Dead* spills through her brain, even though she hasn't read it. But she *knows* it, she knows everything.

She knows that the last destination of every impulse, no matter what twisted or frustrated route it might take, is to cut through the crap to the purity of emptiness experienced during your first minutes in the world. She laughs at how ridiculously obvious this is.

"I'm here," Tom says.

She is almost up at the ceiling now. She tries to touch it. Her arm is as long as a highway, red-checkered. Fire ripples out of her fingers.

"Oh," she says.

"Go with the flow," Tom says, his voice a thousand pianos.

During the night his mother and father apparently return home and go to bed. Tom points out their galoshes in the hallway closet when Lou is leaving.

"Shit," Lou whispers, only now remembering that he *has* parents.

"Ah, they were probably blotto," he says. Then he tells her to wait, and he runs back downstairs, returning with the suitcase she'd brought so that their father would think she was going to a pajama party.

"Oh, yeah," she says, taking the case. He kisses her softly on the lips, and she floats out the door.

It's very cold. The sun has just risen, and the sky is the flat grey of a switched-off TV screen. The bungalows along the street squat and gleam and steam like kettles.

She remembers that she and Tom kissed a lot. Suddenly they both had their clothes off and were kissing but always stopping because of getting distracted. There was no self-consciousness. His penis was hard sometimes, and sometimes it wasn't. She remembers it descending on her from a great height, and her pointing to her crotch, and both of them gaping at the writhing snakes that her pubic hair looked like.

It wasn't frightening. None of it was. All night he talked in John Lennon's voice. At one point she asked him to sing "A Day in the Life," and he did. At one point they dropped the other half tab.

They kissed, and he ran his hands over her body, and they were both naked. But—it only now dawns on her—she can't remember if they went all the way. She stops walking and concentrates on how she feels down there. But her whole body seems anesthetized. Maybe she's sore, maybe she isn't. She can't tell.

Their mother is the only one up. She's watching a test pattern on TV, and dropping on the floor at her feet, Lou gets caught up in watching it with her.

Their mother seizes Lou's hand, something she does every time Lou goes near her these days. Their mother's tiny, smooth hand is a child's. Her white hair is an old lady's. Her tight hold on Lou's hand is like a child's or an old lady's.

Bringing their mother's hand down before her eyes, Lou studies it, enraptured, in love with every pore and fine line. You'd never know by their mother's hand that she grew up on a farm. It was probably her two older brothers who did all the chores. Their mother has said that she thought the sun rose and set on her brothers. One of them was named Jim. Lou thinks that he's who their mother named the baby after, and it was a coincidence that her husband had the same name. Although maybe because of being surrounded by Jims (it was also her father's name) their mother just felt that a male baby had to be called Jim. You can't talk to their mother about babies. Or about her brothers dying in the war. She pretends not to hear. Another thing you can't talk to her about is her hair going white overnight.

Lou looks up at her hair. Her hair is her, Lou thinks. Pure and white. A surprise of whiteness that Lou suddenly feels mirrored inside herself as the one unsullied thing she has harbored no matter what. Inside Lou the surprise of whiteness is that she has been mad at everyone but never at their mother. How could she be? Lou thinks that this whiteness, this absence of anger, will get her into heaven.

"Are you happy?" she asks their mother, reaching up and touching the white hair to touch the purity inside herself. She wants their mother to be blissful.

"Oh, yes," their mother answers, and the two of them watch the test pattern again.

But after a minute their mother says, "Every once in a while, though, I yearn for the most terrible thing to happen."

The test pattern turns into razor lines, prison bars made of razor blades. Lou lets go of their mother's hand.

"Some days," their mother says, "I want to be on the brink of a terrible thing."

Lou comes to her feet. Why is their mother telling her this? Lou has forgotten asking their mother if she is happy. "I have to go to the bathroom," Lou mutters, leaving the room.

In the bathroom Lou remembers the other purity, the one she despises. She pulls down her jeans and underpants and inserts two fingers into herself. There's no obstacle.

All New Year's Day Lou has living-color dreams of babies. If the dreams represent pregnancy fears they are the only time until she misses her period that the prospect of pregnancy crosses her mind.

The next day, at her suggestion, she and Tom make out during their lunch period in the same beat-up red Volkswagen that he dragged her to when she stabbed the knife into the vice-principal's door. Their breath quickly fogs the windows, concealing them, but she would have taken off her blouse anyway. His unexpected cautiousness ("Better not," he says when she starts undoing her buttons) only makes her more reckless. Tearing the last button free, she throws her head back and laughs to be acting so wanton.

Almost every day after school they go down to his basement. He tells his mother that they're working on a chemistry project so not to worry if she smells smoke. They light up a joint, and invariably it's up to Lou to get things started, but as soon as she does, he takes right over. He ejaculates on her stomach. One time she has an orgasm, and it's then, just as he withdraws, seeing the evidence of his orgasm.

"I love you," she tells him.

"I know," he answers, and she thinks he means that it goes without saying he loves her back.

She is so happy! She is nice to everybody—she *wants* to be—while being her true wild self with Tom. At last! What a relief not to have to try to impress him any longer! She stops reading every book he reads and admits to him it was only a ruse. Anything that enters her head, she says. He sometimes looks shocked, but he's never put off. "Let's go back to my place," he says. Afterward they have tea in the kitchen, served by his mother, a drab, frowning, old-fashioned-looking woman in a housedress and apron, who seems to have been warned by someone in another room to act normal. When they sit down at the table, she always comes out with something that sounds as if she's on to them: "You can't give it your best without nourishment." "You've earned this, I imagine." But Tom says she's as thick as two boards. Once she's poured their tea, she leaves them alone.

Lou would like to tell Tom's mother the truth. The last thing she feels is bad. In fact, she feels the opposite: holy, because love is flowing out of her, in all directions. Even their father she loves. She recalls how he was when he had Lovergirls, how he seemed, then, to be in the same mood that she is in now, and it occurs to her that he must have been in love with all of those women to act so happy and nice.

Of course Lou doesn't tell Tom's mother the truth. She doesn't tell a soul, except Sherry, who thinks she and Tom have been doing it for months anyway.

"When do I get to meet him?" Sherry asks.

Lou taps her teeth with a fingernail she no longer bites. Before the acid trip the fact that she had a school drop-out for a best friend was one of the secrets she kept from Tom. Now she likes to see him surprised. "We'll come by your work," she says.

They go there the next day. In the lobby they stuff their pockets with the free cigarettes that are lying around in silver cases for golf-club members. The promise of this is how Lou got Tom to come anywhere near what he calls a capitalist temple. Tom also takes a handful of matches. Then they go down a green-shag-carpeted hallway with overhead lights like giant golf balls.

"This better not take long," Tom mutters.

Since it's off-season, the bar is almost empty. In the gloom Sherry stands out like a spotlit entertainer. She calls "It's okay!" to a man with a brush cut, who has demanded identification. "They're my friends!" she calls. She hurries over to them.

Seeing her through Tom's eyes, Lou can't believe that this bouffant blonde in the tight low-cut white dress and white high-heeled go-go boots is anyone she remotely knows. She turns traitor. As they follow Sherry to a table, she looks over her shoulder at Tom. "Think of it as a freak show," she whispers.

Sherry goes back to the bar and returns with three glasses of Coke on a tray.

"Spiked?" Lou asks.

Sherry sighs. "There's some dumb regulation that I'm not allowed to pour. Can you believe it?"

Lou looks over at the man with the brush cut. "I thought my father was the last holdout," she says.

"I hope it doesn't mean your father's a premature ejaculator," Sherry says. "Because that's what Gino is."

Tom's laugh is embarrassed.

"No, he *is,*" Sherry says seriously. "It's really a hang-up for him. It's really sad."

"Sherry has a heart of gold," Lou explains, standing and leaning forward so that Tom can reach his match to her cigarette. Somehow she's across the wide table while he and Sherry are beside each other on a plush leather loveseat.

"Talk," Sherry says to Tom. "I want to hear your accent."

"For Christ's sake," Lou says, because Tom hates having his accent pointed out. But he smiles at Sherry and says that he's more popular than Jesus Christ.

"Oh, remember?" Sherry cries. "That got the Beatles in so much shit, remember? God." She turns to face Tom, a shift of position that deepens her cleavage. "I can't believe it. It's like having John Lennon right here in The Nineteenth Hole. I mean—" she looks at Lou, "for you it must be like going to bed with John Lennon."

Lou's eyes are on Tom, whose eyes are on Sherry's tits.

Sherry changes the subject to listing anyone she's slept with who is vaguely well known: the guy who owns the Chevrolet dealership down the street, the guy who does the helicopter traffic reports on the radio. For the first time in months Lou feels spite. She hates the feeling, but she can't keep it out. She wants to catch Tom's eye, to make Sherry a joke between them, but he's in a slack-jawed staring trance.

Eventually Lou can't stand it. She gets up and heads straight for the bar. Like she owns the place, she goes around behind to the bottles and pours vermouth into a beer mug. The bartender stays facing the other way, talking to somebody. Lou has two gulps, refills the mug, then takes it back to the table. "Here," she says, plunking down in front of Tom, jolting him and Sherry out of intense conversation.

"What's this?" he asks.

"Booze," Lou says. "Free and contraband." She sits on the arm of the loveseat.

Tom takes a sip, smiles and raises the glass, toasting the air between her and Sherry.

He has a mysterious smile on his face all the way home. Lou can't get an acknowledgement out of him that Sherry is either cheap or stupid.

"I thought you were her friend," he smiles, wagging his finger.

"I am!"

He doesn't ask her to come into his house.

He doesn't show up for school. She phones him. "He's at school," his mother says. The day after that he says, "You're not my jailer," when Lou demands to know where he was. Walking home, they don't talk. Because she senses what is about to happen, she clings to his arm, which he holds so rigidly she feels sick with humiliation and loss. But she doesn't let go. At the turnoff to his house he stops.

"Am I coming to your place?" she asks. She has to ask it.

He looks directly at her. "In some things," he says, "you are absolutely innocent."

"You fucking bastard," she cries. She slaps his face and runs away, her head roaring with fury. She will shoot him.

She gets the gun and conducts a mad search of the bomb shelter for bullets. After forty-eight hours of dread, the truth is exhilarating. Except for revenge she feels as if she's completely over him.

The bullets are nowhere to be found. Their fuck-up of a father probably only ever had one, and he shot his foot with it. Lou sits on one of the bunks and regards her thin, cold-reddened thighs and lets out a sob. Nothing seems more pathetic than her inability to kill.

Up in the house she calls Sherry, who denies sleeping with Tom, then confesses and apologizes all over the place, then says she had a lousy time, then says she wouldn't do it again if she was paid to.

"You are my enemy," Lou tells her coldly. She calls Tom, intending to tell him the same thing, but the first words out of her mouth are, "You're not a fucking bastard."

He says he is. He says it's over.

"I don't care about Sherry," she lies.

"Sherry has nothing to do with it." He lets out a long sigh. "Look, I just don't love you."

"You don't have to."

"I'm very sorry."

"Every word of this conversation is a small death," she says. "Enough small deaths constitute dying."

"You cannot die," he says.

She detects a ray of light. "I don't want to," she says, her voice cracking.

"Even though your body is cut into pieces," he says, and she realizes he is quoting from *The Tibetan Book of the Dead,* "you will recover."

"You fucking bastard!" she cries, slamming down the phone.

· · ·

Not since the baby carriage was hit by a car has Lou cried, and not since Rapunzel went through the fan belt has she cried in front of anyone. Rapunzel is the only time that Norma knows about. She sits on the edge of Lou's bed and strokes Lou's hair, down to her waist. Lou's crying doesn't sound like someone crying. If their mother is paying any attention, she's going to think one of them has gone into labor or something. Halfway down Lou's back, Norma spreads her fingers. They almost reach either side, that's how thin Lou is. But Lou is as hard as a board. When Norma was small, for reassurance she liked to lay her hand on Lou's hard, straight back. What Sandy liked to do was to lay her ear on an empty dinner plate.

"Bastard!" Lou cries. That's all she's said so far. Bastard, fucking bastard. Since their father isn't home, it must be Tom. Norma finds herself a bit staggered to realize that Lou was probably sleeping with Tom, if she is this upset.

"I never trusted that guy," Norma says passionately, which is true, though based entirely on the fact that his glasses are tinted. She looks at the bedside clock. A quarter to six and she hasn't started dinner. "Dad's going to be home soon," she warns without much hope.

But in another minute the desperate, gasping cries stop, and Lou rolls over onto her back. "I'm nothing now," she says. "I've got nobody."

"You've got me," Norma says. "And Sandy." She pauses. "And Mom." Lou's hand drops on Norma's thigh, and Norma feels the wrist for a pulse. The truth is, she knows what Lou means. Who would *she* be if Stella didn't want to be her friend anymore? Oh, just the thought makes her light-headed!

"Am I alive?" Lou asks dully.

"As far as I can tell." With her thumb and forefinger Norma encircles Lou's tiny wrist. Measuring again. It has amazed her all her life that Lou is her sister.

After dinner Norma walks to Stella's house. It's warm for February, and windy. Norma finds herself overcome with happiness. How can she be happy when Lou has a broken heart? But she is. The wind carries her along, and she feels herself to be things she knows she is not—light as a feather, fascinating, unpredictable—and crossing the schoolyard, she just has to open her arms and run.

"Guess what?" Stella greets her at the door. "My parents are out."

Stella also seems to be in a strange, high mood. Her hair is pinned up in big, spectacular loops, and she's wearing white lipstick and slashes of rouge. She wants to do something crazy. "I know," she says. "Let's get drunk!"

Norma stares at her.

"Oh." Stella looks crestfallen. "Don't you want to?"

Norma can't speak. She's just thought of something she hasn't thought about in years: that time she and Lou tied their mother with a skipping rope.

Before she recovers, Stella perks up and starts dragging her by the arm. "Okay, I have a better idea."

They go into the living room, and Stella turns on the radio. "Let's dance!" she cries.

Because the music is some old rock and roll song, they start to jive. Norma, who learned how from their mother, leads. Stella is all loose-limbed and clumsy. She smiles flirtatiously. At the beginning of the next song, "I'm a Believer," she squeals and runs over to turn up the volume. Then she runs back and stands in front of Norma, shaking her long body like a mop.

"Come on!" she cries. "Shimmy!"

Norma does a more moderate version. This wild Stella is overwhelming. Maybe she already is drunk. Pins fly from her hair, loosening loops that fall like ticker tape. Both of them laugh every time another pin flies out. Stella screams with laughter.

At the end of the song they collapse on the couch. Then Stella jumps right back up again, crying "Cherish!" She yanks Norma's hand. "I love this song," she cries.

It's a slow dance. Norma tries to lead them in a box step. But Stella can't follow and loses patience. "Let's just dance normally," she says, and moving closer she drops her head on Norma's shoulder.

They keep their feet in one place and sway. Norma's heart works like a piston, like a heart for both of them, where their breasts touch. When the song is over, news comes on, and Stella turns the dial, trying to find more music to dance to, then gives up and switches the radio off. Norma is still swept away. She lowers herself onto the edge of the couch.

"*The Man I Love*," Stella reads from the *TV Guide*. " 'A nightclub singer is in love with a pianist who is in love with a society woman.' Let's watch that, okay?" Norma nods. Stella turns on the TV, drops a cushion onto Norma's lap and curls up on the couch with her head on the cushion. "I always use my mom for a pillow," she explains.

After a minute Norma pulls out the pins holding Stella's two remaining loops. Combing her fingers through Stella's hair reminds her of Lou crying on the bed.

She combs Stella's beautiful hair and curls it around her fingers. A couple of times Stella gets up—to go to the bathroom and to bring them Cokes and cookies—but she lies back down on Norma's lap. Presently she falls asleep. Norma strokes her hair so lightly that it will seem like a breeze.

She feels suspended in a supreme and clairvoyant point in her life. She feels that she has crossed over every murky, base desire to get here. The height of her life is now. She is having her turn now.

Soon it will be Stella's turn. This thought comes gradually to Norma, partly inspired by the love triangle in the movie. Stella will get a boyfriend soon. Next year at university. But it's okay. Only a couple of hours ago the idea of losing Stella was unbearable. Now it's okay, because from the height of her life Norma can see that Stella getting a boyfriend is inevitable and overdue. Stella will get married and be happy forever. From beginning to end, Stella's life will be perfect. Some lives are meant to be perfect. Obviously there have to be some lives against which the rest—her own life, Lou's life—are measured.

Lou. If a phone was within reach, Norma would call Lou up right now. She would say . . . what would she say? Not "You've got me" again, although it's what she wants to tell her, really meaning it now. No, she'd say something that sounds closer to the truth—the tenderness and amazement she felt, feeling the beat of blood in Lou's tiny wrist.

Around the end of March it occurs to Lou that she hasn't had a period in over a month. She's not worried. The one time she isn't certain that Tom pulled out is New Year's Eve, and she's had a period since then.

In the middle of April she urinates into an empty pickle jar and takes the bus to a drugstore that has a big, handpainted window sign announcing "PREGNACY TESTS! RESULTS IN 2 HOURS!" The misspelling of pregnancy and the exclamation marks suggest to her someone easy-going and grateful for business. Not that she gives a shit what an illiterate pharmacist thinks.

She waits the two hours in a restaurant, drinking coffee in the booth by the window. Every other passerby seems to be a mother with a baby or young children. Most of the babies are crying, and all the children that aren't acting up look miserable. All the mothers that don't look vindictive look tranquilized.

When she goes back to the drugstore, the pharmacist flips through a tray of cards and reads aloud last names: "Ferguson, Farquar, Feldman. . . ." Are these all women having pregnancy tests? "Field," he says finally. "Negative."

"Oh," Lou says. "Oh, shit."

The pharmacist doesn't look much older than she is, and his hair is long for a pharmacist, curling over his collar. "Negative," he says, giving her the once-over, "is good news."

She misses another period. Her breasts are swollen and attracting second glances, and in the morning she craves Twinkies so badly she skips school to go to the store and buy them.

"I'm obviously pregnant," she tells herself. And yet she's obviously not. Even if the urine test was wrong, and even if Tom didn't always pull out soon enough, she can't imagine her body letting that bastard's sperm in. It's not some romantic idea she entertains that babies have to be born of love. It's that her insides seize up at the thought of him. It's that thinking of him and Sherry together, she has brought up bile.

On the third of May she goes for another test. Having failed to find an empty or near-empty jar or small bottle, she has urinated into a whiskey bottle. "Believe it or not I think this is the second today," the pharmacist says, checking out the Canadian Club label.

She tests positive. It's the young, long-haired pharmacist who gives her the news. He says positive is always a sure thing, and the reason she came up negative before was probably a combination of it being too early to tell and her urine being diluted.

She nods. Although there are people lined up behind her, she can't move away. She stands there looking at the pharmacist, waiting for the entire textbook explanation of how she has come to this point in her life.

The pharmacist reaches for a pad and jots something down, then rips off the page, rolls it up and hands it to her like a joint.

"Give this guy a call," he says quietly. "This guy's cool."

As if what he wrote might fall out, as if the piece of paper contains her one hope, which it does, she continues holding it the way he gave it to her. Suddenly she feels nine months pregnant. There is a baby inside of her, but what it feels like is a malignant tumor. She's in shock at the thought that with every second it is replicating its cells.

A pay phone is in the restaurant, outside the washrooms. The abortionist's name is Dr. Dickey. She pictures a homo. Twice she gets a busy signal, and then she is struck by a wave of nausea and has to go into the Ladies and sit on the toilet, her head between her knees.

How can she be pregnant? That bastard. She should tell him. Scare the shit out of him. At school he strides right past her. The only time he has even looked at her was last week. He was coming toward her, outside the cafeteria, and because he slowed down and shook his head, she was sure he was gathering the courage to finally speak to her. But when he was a few feet away, she knew that he was stoned, that's all, that he hadn't seen her yet. She went up to him, forcing him to stop. God knows what got into her, but she grabbed one of his hands, yanked it up and down a couple of times, as if she were cranking an engine, and called him an asshole. He looked worried and annoyed. A few hours later they passed in the hall again, and he threw her that mad-eyed, sideways glance you get from a dog in a hurry.

She should tell him. Watch him sweat. The idea grows on her and banishes her nausea. She leaves the cubicle. In the mirror above the sink she investigates her face. Somewhere she's read that pregnancy is good for your complexion. She bets Tom would marry her, do the hypocritical thing. When they stole cigarettes ("liberated" them, he said) and had to get out of the store fast, he held the door open for ladies. An English gentleman bullshit revolutionary.

What if she married him? She steps back and stares at herself, imagining herself with white, milk-huge breasts, a little baby in her arms, and Tom compelled to love her.

She can see that. Yes, she would like that. She leaves the washroom and the restaurant. On the sidewalk she brushes against a man who growls, "Watch where you're going!" The effect is like a hypnotist snapping his fingers. She hurries back into the restaurant and down to the phone. What's happening, she tells herself, fishing in her pockets for the dime, is that her hormones are sending up tempting messages. Her hormones are trying to trick her.

The abortionist's line is still busy.

"God fucking damn it," she says, banging down the receiver. She regards her stomach. It looks twice as big as it did fifteen minutes ago. It looks evil, like a punishment. It looks like the great multiplication of her sorrows.

That Sandy doesn't have the flu or swollen glands but is pregnant strikes her from out of nowhere and as the truth at last. There are other facts she could face. Two weeks ago she bled, and she's never had an orgasm, which up until now she thought you had to, to conceive—she could go on believing that—but the minute the idea of a baby enters her mind, she knows that her body has been claimed. All she wants to do is cup her stomach. She goes home early from school to cup it in private.

The next morning she pees in a whiskey bottle and takes it to a drugstore that she's noticed from the bus on account of its big pregnancy-test sign. She isn't uncertain, and she doesn't need confirmation. She goes to the drugstore because she assumes that you're supposed to. Then you go to a pediatrician. From here on in she is dedicated to doing what a mother-to-be is supposed to do.

Already she loves her baby so much! The first thing she intends to tell the pediatrician is, if you have to choose between the baby and me, let the baby live. Having it inside her feels exactly like a miracle, as if an angel touched her stomach and a baby began to grow.

She can hardly think of Dave being involved. Of course she'll marry him now, but there's no reason she has to tell him why right away. It's hard to connect him, grunting and pumping and sweating on top of her, either with a baby or with herself. When she was a virgin, she didn't know how that felt. Now she knows. Now, with a baby inside her, she feels clean through and through.

"Miss Jones?" the pharmacist says.

Sandy gave a false name. "Yes," she says.

"Positive. You're pregnant."

"Yes, I know." She stands there until it's clear he's not going to tell her anything else.

Except for lying on her bed with her hands on her stomach, she doesn't want to do anything. The truth keeps overwhelming her. Her eyes fill, and she swears to God she'll be a good mother. She'd like to tell Norma. After she has the pregnancy test, that night, she longs to climb into Norma's bed like she used to and whisper the news.

But what if Norma is shocked? Sandy's pretty sure that Norma hasn't even kissed a boy yet. And what if Lou wakes up and demands to know what the two of them are talking about? Lou will call her a stupid idiot for not being careful. She won't say "pregnant," she'll say "knocked up." She might start yelling and wake their father. Phone up Dave, yell at him. Who knows what Lou might do?

Near dawn Sandy hears their mother in the TV room, and she gets out of bed and goes in to join her. Their mother gives her a sleepy smile and lifts the blanket for her to cover herself. A strong smell of their mother is under the blanket. It's like an old picture of her, or seeing her tap shoes. Tomorrow night is her bath night. Wednesdays after dinner she brings her coffee mug and the kitchen radio into the bathroom and soaks in the tub, listening to a big-band program. Over the years the night and length of her bath have changed a couple of times because the program has. Sandy remembers that when she was little, their mother sang along with the music.

"Can't sleep?" their mother asks, squeezing Sandy's hand.

Sandy shakes her head. Their mother doesn't let go of her hand, she's so glad to have company. None of them sits with her on the couch anymore, Sandy realizes guiltily. When they watch TV, they sit on one of the chairs, or they lie on the floor. The couch seems to be their mother's, Sandy tells herself, their mother's private place—that's the reason.

On the TV the test pattern flickers off, and the words "THIS IS ONLY A TEST" appear, accompanied by a pulsing beep sound.

"In case of emergency," their mother explains, releasing Sandy's hand and picking up her mug from the side table. "Such as nuclear war."

Sandy sees herself running with her baby through fiery explosions to the bomb shelter. She slips her hands under the blanket and gently presses her stomach.

When their mother was pregnant with her, did she love her this much? Sandy can't bear to think so, can't bear it for their mother's sake, because if she did, no matter how much Sandy ever loved her, their mother's love was unrequited. Sandy lays her head on their mother's shoulder. When was the last time she even *thought* of their mother? "Mommy?" she says.

"Hmm?"

"You know what? I'm pregnant."

The beeping on the TV stops. Sandy straightens to see their mother's face. Their mother is still looking at the TV. She is frowning, and for a second Sandy is confused. Then she remembers that their mother doesn't like talk about babies, and she is more confused. There must be exceptions. Her baby isn't just any baby.

Their mother looks at her. "Are you going to have an abortion?" she asks sternly.

"No," Sandy says. She is shocked.

Their mother pats Sandy's leg. "Good."

"I have a boyfriend. I'm going to marry him. Daddy met him. Did he tell you? Daddy likes him." Their mother smiles. "But don't tell Daddy anything yet," Sandy adds anxiously. "Okay? I haven't told him."

"When you have an abortion," their mother says, "your body goes into mourning." Her eyes are back on the TV. Her voice is back to being kind and soft.

"But, Mommy, I'm not going to have one."

"Your heart breaks. Your tear ducts won't close. Your hair follicles act up. Your hair just gives up." She looks at Sandy again. "You can't trick nature. You can't dance to the music and then kill the piper."

On Saturday morning Sandy is being sick to her stomach in the fabric store washroom, when she is overcome with a superstitious feeling that not telling Dave will rebound on her baby. That her baby will be born deformed! She leaves work and goes straight to the hardware store, right through to the back, where Dave is fixing a toaster.

"Princess!" he greets her happily.

His big jaw drops at the news. He nods that they should keep it a secret and that they should marry sometime in July and tell everyone afterward.

"I'll make all its baby clothes," Sandy says, talking to herself. "I'll buy the material now. As long as I'm still working at the store, I can get a twenty percent discount."

At home, as she's hanging up her coat, she sees Lou lying on the living-room chesterfield. Just lying there on her back, without a book and with her hands folded across her chest, her eyes fixed on the ceiling. "Are you sick?" Sandy asks her.

Lou slowly turns her head. "I almost died." She sounds proud.

"What?" Sandy goes over to her.

"A quack almost killed me."

"What do you mean?"

Lou looks back at the ceiling. "But here I am. And this is my room. And you're all here. And there's no place like home."

Sandy sighs. "I don't get this joke," she says. "Because you don't look very good, you know. You're white as a ghost."

"But I *feel* good," Lou says fiercely, smiling. "Why did Dorothy leave Oz to go back to Kansas? I've been lying here trying to figure that out. What's she got back in Kansas? A wrecked house, poverty, no friends for miles. And Elmira Gultch is still going to take Toto to the pound. That hasn't changed."

"Auntie Em," Sandy says. "She misses Auntie Em."

Lou throws back her head. "Ha!" Her thin white throat reminds Sandy of how frail her baby is. "That old bitch," Lou says. She imitates Auntie Em's voice. "I know three farm hands that'll be out of a job before long." Her eyes are so eager, so rapturous that Sandy walks away from her, over to the window. "Auntie Ems," Lou cries, "are one of the biggest weapons the mortal coil has!"

Sandy looks out the window, aligning herself with the green grass, the little red maple covered in buds, the robin on the fire hydrant—all the signs of spring in their front yard.

VITAL DISCONNECTION

1969

No one hears their mother leave the house and push up the creaking garage door. All the windows are open, but everyone sleeps through the clanging of the aluminum ladder being carried to the other side of the house and dropped against the eaves.

Pigeons running around on the roof sound like gangs of women in stiletto heels. How did their mother move so quietly up there? On the day of her funeral the three girls argue about it. Everything—the mystery of their mother's whole life—seems to boil down to how she crossed right over their heads without waking them. She just tiptoed. She crawled. She slid, seated along the peak. She walked along the peak like a tightrope walker. She could have, she was a dancer! In that wind?

"She floated," offers the drunk, their father, and this shuts them up because naturally they don't believe it, but they can picture it, their mother's long white billowing nightgown. Because it's an angel image.

All the windows are open when their mother goes up on the roof. It's hot and windy, the last day of May, the first hot day. Their father is sleeping in the rollaway down in the basement. At ten past four in the morning he gets up to use the toilet, the downstairs one, and he looks up at the window, which is above the sink, and sees a ladder standing there, outside. He hurries back to the rec room to pull on his trousers. Since his gun is in the bomb shelter, he leaves by the back door.

The police will ask why didn't he glance up at the roof before getting his gun. They won't let him off easy about the gun. He'll say that he thought that he was dealing with a cat burglar. That in the night the face can shine like a light. He'll be precise about when things happened, crediting his-glow-in-the-dark watch, which he wears to bed, and his habit of frequently noting the time. An old military habit, he'll say.

At four-thirty-five he wakes Lou and Norma. He speaks softly from their bedroom door. Their mother is on the roof and won't come down unless she has whiskey. He wants Norma to take a bottle up to her. He says he tried to but with his bad foot he couldn't climb.

"What's she doing on the roof?" Norma asks, patting the bedside table for her glasses.

Lou gets out of bed, goes to the window and raises the blind. "Hey, I can see her shadow," she cries, pointing to the neighbor's lawn.

"Keep your voice down," their father hisses. "We don't want the whole street in on this. We don't want a big production."

Sandy opens her bedroom door as they're hurrying by. Norma explains.

"Why has he got his gun?" asks Sandy, the first to notice.

"Hurry up," their father says.

Outside, the wind whips their pajama legs. It whips and lifts Sandy's and Lou's long hair and streams back their mother's white hair. There she is, sitting beside the chimney, holding on to it with one hand and on to the roof with her other hand. She is vividly white and unreal, like a cutout.

"Jesus Christ," Lou says with a laugh.

"Keep it down," their father rasps.

"How long has she been up there?" Norma asks.

"I don't know," he mutters. "All night. I don't know."

"Mommy," Sandy calls quietly, waving.

"But what's she doing up there?" Norma asks again. She is thinking of the time their mother wanted to go on the roof because there was no whiskey in the house.

"How the hell should I know?" their father says. He thrusts the bottle at her. "Okay, there's two fingers' worth here. Let her have it, then get her down. Tell her if she wants more, she has to come and get it."

He puts his gun on the grass to hold the ladder steady as Norma climbs. The wind whistles. Stepping onto the roof, Norma is almost blown backward. She drops awkwardly into a crouch, which causes her glasses to fly off. They slide into the eavestrough.

"Leave them," their father whisper-yells.

Their mother turns her head in Norma's direction. Norma can

only make out the slow swivel of their mother's head and her face like the moon.

Down below, their father hunches against the wind to light a cigarette. Lou takes the opportunity to dart up the ladder. "Hey!" he growls, making a grab for her leg.

But she is already out of his reach. She laughs. If she were still pregnant, she'd probably be too out of kilter, too middle-heavy to climb ladders.

"She won't let go," Norma says when Lou reaches them. Norma is sitting beside their mother and holding the bottle at their mother's mouth.

Lou moves over to the chimney and stands there, looking at their father and Sandy looking up. The little orange flare when their father inhales his cigarette strikes her as an assault. Pitiful. She has an urge to spit on him. "It's great up here," she says. She laughs again, exhilarated.

"She had that nightmare," Norma says. "That's why she came up."

"Which nightmare!" Lou tosses her head back to feel her hair blow. It's not so dark that she can't see the clouds. They gallop over her. The clouds seem to be what's making the wind.

"You know," Norma says. "The one she had in the bomb shelter."

"Yeah, but I never knew what it was about."

Their mother speaks. "Suffocation," she says in a frightened voice. "No air. A terrible weight. A terrible urge."

Now Lou notices how rigidly their mother is sitting. "You better get down," she says, worried for the first time.

"I can't." She indicates with a nod at Norma that she wants another drink.

"There's none left," Norma says gently. "You have to come down, Mom."

Their mother shakes her head.

"Lou! Lou!" It's their father, calling hoarsely through cupped hands.

"She's too scared to come down," Lou shouts.

"Shut up!" he shouts. He checks the time on his watch, then takes a step back and bumps into Sandy. Sandy hurries away from him, but it is only to get another view of their mother. She is torn between their mother and her unborn baby, between going up to help their mother and not taking any foolish risks.

"You better phone the fire department," Lou shouts as loudly as before.

"I'll phone," Sandy offers.

"No!" their father shouts. He throws down his cigarette. "Okay," he says, whisper-yelling. "Everybody calm down. Everybody shut up and calm down. Lou, you get in front of your mother. Norma, you get behind her. Crawl to the ladder together. Take it easy."

"I can't," their mother moans.

"What if you had more whiskey?" Norma asks her.

"No. You go. Leave me." She bows her head. Her hand slips down the chimney.

"Jesus." Crouching, Lou plants her hand over their mother's. "Hold on," she says. Their mother's toes are curled like a little bird's. Lou calls down to their father: "Phone the fire department! She can't hold on much longer!"

"Goddamn it, keep your voice down!"

"PHONE THE FUCKING FIRE DEPARTMENT!"

Their father flails around as if expecting to see all the neighborhood lights switch on. Across the street one does.

"Daddy . . . ," Sandy pleads.

"All right, that's it." Their father scoops up his gun and points it at the roof. "Mary," he calls to their mother, "come down right now, or I start shooting."

"For Christ's sake," Lou snorts.

Their mother begins to stand but can't and sits back down, hard.

"Don't move," Norma says, grabbing their mother's arm. Their mother is shaking. "He's just trying to scare you. We'll phone the fire department."

"At the count of ten," their father calls.

"*I'll* phone," Lou says to their mother and Norma.

"One . . . ," their father says, and then, "Hey," to Lou, who is scrambling down the ladder. When she touches ground, she pushes the gun barrel away from her.

"Look," he says. His face is gullied with shadows. "I'm not going to shoot, for Christ's sake." Lou runs to the front door. "Where are you going?" he yells. "You better not phone!"

Sandy comes up behind him. "Daddy. . . ."

His arm swings out and hits her across the neck, knocking her backward onto the grass. She cries "Oh!" in surprise. He gapes at her, his arm still horizontal, the gun at the end of it aimed at the house. "Go get Lou here," he says.

Sandy sits up and cups her stomach. She is so concerned about the jolt to her baby that she is on the brink of saying so. Spilling the beans.

Up on the roof their mother has come to her feet. She clings to the chimney. The wind is caught under her nightgown and swells her up.

Norma, still sitting, has a hold of their mother's ankle and can feel that she is steady, no longer shaking. She doesn't know whether to urge her to stay put or to climb down. "Don't look down," she warns.

Without glasses, Norma sees only that their mother's head is lowered. She doesn't see their mother's final countenance. Their mother squirms her foot, and Norma thinks this means she wants to climb down. So Norma lets go of her. In a balletic, yielding motion their mother's arms lift. Then they make slow, backwards circles, signifying, Norma realizes a half-second too late, that she has lost her balance.

On her way down everyone but their mother cries out. Her hand brushes Sandy's arm. When she hits the grass, there is the faintest thud. She lands on her back. Sandy drops down beside her. Their father drops down on her other side, grabs her shoulders, listens for her heart, checks his watch, begins mouth to mouth. The girls cover their own mouths with their hands. They don't ask if she's dead. By her eyes, they know. Even Norma, down on the ground now but without her glasses, can see that their mother's wide-open eyes are dead.

The fire engine arrives, siren blaring. "She went up to rescue the cat," their father tells the fireman who kneels beside him.

Neighbors have come over in pajamas and nightgowns and hair

curlers. The man from two doors down says, "*Our* cat?" because his is the only house that has a cat, on this street, anyway.

"*Our* cat," their father says. "We just got it."

More sirens are approaching. The fireman who is examining their mother sits back on his heels and rubs a hand down his face. Another fireman spots their father's gun at the foot of the ladder and goes to pick it up, then doesn't. Norma asks this fireman if she can get her glasses out of the eavestrough, and he looks with suspicion at her and at the gun, then back at her before telling her to make it snappy.

The wind dies. There is the calmness of dawn. Everyone, including their father, talks in undertones. To all the questions the police ask, he comes up with passable lies. The girls nod corroboration. When their father goes off in the ambulance, they decline offers of help from women neighbors.

Inside the house Norma turns on the TV and makes breakfast. They eat in the kitchen, with the test-pattern hum in the background, as if it's any early morning. Lou says that you could see Mrs. Kent's droopy tits through her negligee and that Mr. Albee, the man who asked if it was his cat, knew their father was bullshitting.

After breakfast Norma decides to vacuum. She has a hard time aiming the plug into the outlet. She hears Lou telling Sandy to take the day off work. "I'm on commission," Sandy says, and Lou says, "They'll pay you anyway. For Christ's sake, our mother just died."

Norma lets go of the vacuum cord. When she straightens up, the room spins. She goes into the kitchen, where her sisters are. "Our mother just died," she says. Lou and Sandy seem far away and tiny. They look at her as if she has spoken in a foreign language. "I think I'll leave the vacuuming," she says, falling onto a chair.

Midmorning their father returns, wearing another man's shirt. "Call your Aunt Betty," he says, clutching Norma's shoulder as he passes her. He takes a bottle of whiskey out of the cupboard and disappears into their mother's bedroom.

Lou makes the call. "I'll be right there!" Aunt Betty screams. "Don't bother," Lou says to the dial tone. As soon as she hangs up, the phone rings. It's a reporter asking if their mother is the same Mary Field who dropped her baby over Niagara Falls. "No," Lou says and slams down the receiver.

A minute later another reporter calls and asks the same question.

"Here's your headline," Lou says. "Grieving daughter suggests to homo reporter that he go fuck himself."

Aunt Betty is accompanied by a reporter with whom she seems to be on friendly terms. Lou shoves the man back out the door and turns the lock. "What did you tell him?" she demands of her aunt.

"What could I tell him?" Aunt Betty screams. "What do I know? A cat on the roof? You poor things." She spreads her arms and tries to draw Lou and Norma together against her full-length, white mink. Then Sandy emerges from the bathroom, and Aunt Betty rushes over to her and starts crying.

"This is all we need," Lou says to Norma. They don't realize until Aunt Betty lets her go that Sandy is crying, too. She runs back into the bathroom.

Aunt Betty pulls pink Kleenex out of her sleeve and dabs her eyes, which look dry. She sighs at the hole in the wall where their father tossed the vacuum cleaner through. "Where is he?" she asks.

When she has gone to the bedroom, Norma tells Lou that Sandy and Dave are getting married.

"What?" Lou snaps.

"At least that's what Sandy told me yesterday," Norma says. She pushes up her glasses and rubs her eyes. She's still seeing things as if they were far away.

"Is she pregnant?"

"I don't know. I don't think so."

"She must be pregnant. Even *she's* got to know what a fucking moron the guy is. I think she's pregnant. Her tits are bigger."

"Pull yourself together!" Aunt Betty screams at their father.

"Well, anyway," Norma continues, "Dave has gone ahead and rented the Starlight Room."

"Over the shoe repair store?"

Norma nods.

"Nobody rents that," Lou says. "You don't rent that. It's never been rented."

They hear Sandy sobbing in the bathroom. They stare at each other for a minute, then Norma murmurs, "It's good to let it out." She wonders why there doesn't seem to be anything in herself to let out.

Aunt Betty returns, announcing that they're not to worry, she'll take care of everything. The funeral parlor where Uncle Eugene was, she'll book that. Maybe they'll give her a discount for repeat business. She's on her way to the hospital now to make sure everything's been taken care of there. She'll come back for Sandy later. It would be best if Sandy stayed at her house.

No, Lou says in a hard voice. No way. Aunt Betty looks startled. Well, she says, batting her blue-shadowed eyelids, what's the food situation? The same as always, Lou answers. "Look," Lou says, "it's not like a whole lot has changed around here."

"He's a cold-blooded killer and should hang," Lou says.

It's the next morning. She and her sisters are eating breakfast—in Lou's case black coffee and cigarettes. Their father is still asleep. From the heat, from no sleep the night before, from chasing a reporter off the property half an hour ago (GET LOST, GHOULS! she has since written on a piece of paper and taped to the front door), Lou has a headache. "He scared her into standing up," she says, "then he wouldn't call the fire department to get her down. He probably wanted her dead for the insurance money. Lovergirl is probably pestering him to make it legitimate. I should call the police."

"Don't," Norma moans.

"I heard him crying," Sandy says. Her bottom lip quivers.

"Ah, he's pissed," Lou says. She looks speculatively at the phone dangling off the hook.

After lunch Norma walks over to Stella's house. She feels drunk. She meanders. The sun beats down.

Stella and her parents are wearing their clothes from church. All of them answer the door, as though they had been watching for her. Stella's eyes are red. She pulls Norma inside. "We just heard on the radio!" she cries, hugging her. She has on a dress made of white rose-petal shapes sewn together. If Stella's parents weren't there, Norma would run her hand down the petals on Stella's arm. She would allow herself that small consolation.

"Let's go into the living room," Stella's mother says, leading the way.

Stella pulls Norma onto the chesterfield. "You never told me about the baby!" she cries.

"Well, now, Bunny," Stella's father says, "that was before Norma's time."

His eyes are sympathetic, but they hold Norma's. Their message is: "For Stella's sake you must be brave and, if necessary, dishonest."

"I didn't really know about the baby," Norma murmurs.

"But dropping her own baby. It explains why she—" Stella bites her lip. What was she going to say? It explains why their mother drank? Norma didn't think Stella knew about their mother's drinking. Maybe there was something about it on the news.

"Thank God death was instantaneous," Stella's mother says. "Likely the heart stopped during the fall. From fear." She looks pointedly at her daughter. "Which means there'd be *absolutely no pain.*"

Is she talking about Jimmy's death or their mother's? Norma regrets not having listened to the radio.

"We want to do whatever we can to help," Stella's father says.

"Yes, what can we *do?*" Stella asks, her eyes welling.

"I'll make you up a food hamper," Stella's mother says.

"No, it's okay, thanks," Norma says. "We have lots of food." Holding on to the smooth, bone-white arm of the chesterfield is like holding their mother's ankle on the roof. She is going to cry. She stands up. "I have to get back," she says, already heading for the door.

"You just got here!" Stella calls.

"Let her go," Stella's father says.

Stella doesn't. She chases Norma down the driveway and catches her hand. They are both crying, but they walk normally, as if they aren't. Norma keeps squeezing Stella's hand to signal something: gratefulness, sympathy, apology, surprise at Stella pretending to her parents, who are almost certainly watching from the living-room window, that she's not crying, surprise at her guile.

At the end of Stella's street is a little park—a green bus stop bench and a drinking fountain hidden among the only big trees in the subdivision. Today, for a change, there isn't a couple necking on the bench, so Stella and Norma fall onto it. They fall into each other's arms.

Norma can't stop crying. She outcries Stella, who begins to pat her back and say, "I know."

A slight lift of the chin is all it takes for Norma to bring her lips to Stella's. She does it with a sense that she deserves the comfort and that it was bound to happen.

It's a soft, sweet kiss. Norma is delirious with tenderness . . . until Stella starts to draw away, and then Norma won't release her. It's as if a string that has been tugging her all her life is let go.

Stella squeals to have the breath squeezed out of her. Her mouth opens, but at the touch of Norma's tongue, her tongue recoils, her teeth clamp shut. When she jerks her body sideways to escape Norma, that just slides her other breast into Norma's hand. "Stop it!" she screams.

Stella is now standing in front of Norma, violently shaking her head. Her long hair whipping reminds Norma of the night that they did the shimmy. "That's terrible!" Stella cries. "It's sick. Why did you *do* it?"

"I guess I wanted to," Norma says with a serenity that she wonders at herself. Stella wipes her nose on her rose-petal sleeve. She looks reproachful and clueless but prepared to listen. But all Norma can think to say is, "I'm sorry." She doesn't mean she regrets it. She means she's sorry that Stella is so upset. She's sorry that she isn't sorrier or even repelled by herself. She's sorry for transferring her pain, because the fact is she feels a breathtaking relief. She's sorry that pain *is* transferred, like a hot potato.

"But what were you *doing?*" Stella asks petulantly.

Norma shrugs. "I couldn't help it."

"But why? Are you a lesbian or something?"

"I guess so."

Stella looks staggered. "Well—" She bites her bottom lip. In her clear face the transition of her thoughts is touchingly evident. The last thought causes her eyes to fill. "We can't be friends anymore," she says.

"Yeah," Norma sighs. "I know." She adjusted to this months ago. She takes a good last look at Stella. Fairy-tale hair; darling, perfect face; long white hands with pink-painted nails; long, slender legs; knock knees.

"I'm sorry," Stella says. "Your mother just died, but—" She begins to cry, open-mouthed, arms hanging, irresistibly childlike, except that there's nothing Norma can do, and all of a sudden she is anxious to get back home to her sisters. "I'll go so you can stay here for a while," she offers.

"I won't tell anybody," Stella sobs.

The night before the funeral Lou has a dream that their mother is sick in bed. Lou climbs into the bed to hold her, but their mother turns into a mist. In the dream it's obvious to Lou that if she had been a nicer person, their mother would have been proportionately more substantial and not so easily vaporized.

She wakes up crying, still mixed up between the death of their mother and the death of the best part of herself. She buries her face in her pillow and cries for a long time, eventually waking Norma up.

"Are you okay?" Norma asks.

"Yeah."

"I wondered if you were going to cry."

Lou is silent.

"I keep seeing her eyes," Norma says.

When Norma falls back to sleep, Lou starts seeing their mother's eyes, too. Also Tom's, which is like seeing an angel and a devil. It was hopeless, she realizes, expecting Tom to love her, considering that what she loved about him were his cold eyes. She probably got what she deserved. Thank God she had an abortion.

No baby. No mother.

A bird chirps. It must be about five o'clock. The window blind keeps the room dark. Lou folds her arms behind her head. She isn't sad now. It's strange, but she feels a bit high, the way she did on the roof. Even though she knows that their mother was scared up there, she wants to believe that their mother felt like this, that just before she dropped over the edge, or maybe when she was in midair, she felt for a second that, miraculously, she was light enough not to land.

. . .

Norma keeps expecting to feel ashamed but doesn't. When she thinks of Stella, she's only nostalgic for a thing of beauty. She can't bring herself to hate herself. She knows that Stella will survive. One disappointment might even do Stella good. Where before there was no possible obstruction between her heart and Stella, there is now something that feels like the wind blowing back. Not back from Stella. From nowhere, from life—a current of wind in the pure air that was between them.

She tells herself that it's time to forgive their father. But no feeling, of forgiveness or the lack of it, follows the command. Maybe she already has forgiven him, she can't tell. The pity she feels now is because he's so pitiful, drinking, crying at the breakfast table, collapsing anywhere, holing up in their mother's bedroom, fouling himself the night of the funeral—dropping with a barrage of farts onto the pile of towels and sheets that Aunt Betty brought over for some reason and left in the hall.

Norma cleaned him up. At the smell Sandy ran into the bathroom to be sick to her stomach, and Lou said soak him with air-freshener spray and cover him with the sheets. She said, "Can't we get him committed for this?"

All day the three of them watch TV. Sprawled on their mother's couch and on the floor. Their mother's ashes sit on top of the set in what Lou maintains is a used, lacquered cigar box not big enough for all of her.

"Her legs aren't here," Lou decides, confirming Norma's suspicion that they had to cut her legs off to fit her into such a short coffin.

The phone rings a lot, and either Sandy or Norma run to answer it ahead of Lou, who doesn't care who it is, she doesn't ask, she just lifts the receiver, then drops it, leaving it off the hook.

Everyone is worried about the food situation. The day after the funeral Lou calls out, "Tell him to order us some Chinese!" when Norma is talking on the phone to their father's boss, and the boss, hearing Lou, does. From then on Lou makes Norma and Sandy tell anyone who phones that some order-in Chinese would be nice.

Lou won't let anybody in the house, except for their Aunt Betty, who has a key anyway. "We're in mourning," Sandy explains to Dave, and he backs off with the same look of uncertain respect that he used to get when she said, pushing his hand from her leg, "I'm on my period." They kiss by kissing the screen. Through the screen, Sandy finds it possible to tell him she loves him and to think maybe she will someday. She tells him he can announce their engagement now, and she instructs him as to wedding preparations. She opens the door a crack to allow him to pass her the mail, left on the porch on account of the GET LOST, GHOULS! sign. His hand, sliding around the door, is big and hairy and capable—she doesn't forget—of fixing anything you plug in.

On the fourth day after the funeral the principal arrives with ten boxes of groceries collected from a school food drive. "Noticed the sign," he commiserates, as if obviously it's not directed at him. When he realizes it is, when Lou says just leave the boxes on the porch, she'll carry them in, he stares at her for a minute, then punches the palm of his hand and declares that to heck with the rules, what's he going to do for Lou and her sisters is see to it personally that they graduate without having to write final exams.

"That'd help," Lou allows.

Afterward she says to Norma and Sandy, "Let's drag this out for as long as we can."

Norma and Sandy are game, but not because of the free food and the wages without work and the diplomas without exams, and those aren't Lou's real reasons, either. They all have the same feeling of being in a sanctuary together and of keeping vigil.

Every day they come across something, or they think of something, and the anguish, which every day they imagine must be over with, is a small shock. All through the house are reminders, and these are also unexpected, since their mother lived mostly in one room. There are her empties under the stairs, her circular Light Fantastics suitcase in the furnace room, her toothbrush, with bits of food in it, in the bathroom. There are strands of white hair in a comb, and in the clothes hamper there is one of her nightgowns, seeped with the smell of her.

There is the imprint of her mouth on the pieces of toilet paper that she smacked after putting on lipstick Christmas Day. "Bring your Bibles!" Aunt Betty screamed into the phone the night before the funeral. It turned out there was no reason to, and all of them forgot anyway, but right after Aunt Betty called, Sandy took her Bible out of her bottom drawer and found the seven mouths on toilet paper she'd saved and stored between the all-red pages. What made her cry was that every mouth was the same color—"English Rose"—that their mother had only ever had the one tube of lipstick.

Most of the time, though, they don't feel like crying. They feel as if they are waiting for something to happen and as if nothing ever will. This is an inexpressible, deeply, deeply exciting feeling.

After a few days Lou starts calling the TV room "the wake room," because their mother is present in the cigar box and because the empty stacks of Chinese-food containers, the empty Coke bottles, the newspapers and strewn clothes, the full ashtrays make it look as though a party went on there. Not even Norma is inclined to straighten things up. When she has to leave the room, she hurries right back. The sight of the mess and garbage is a relief—a liberation and a kind of compact, or the evidence of a compact, between her and her sisters and their mother.

One morning Sandy's acceptance to the fashion design course at Empire College arrives. It takes her aback. In the wake room they've been studying the photo albums, for the first time in years, and the letter of acceptance has the same effect on Sandy that several of the pictures of herself do. Did she ever look like that? Was she ever that person?

She shows the letter to her sisters, who can't get over her having academic ambitions. "Are you going?" Lou asks. Ever since Tom dumped her, Lou hasn't given a minute's thought to college or university. She feels uncomfortable about this.

"No," Sandy answers. Her twinge of guilt is entirely over Mrs. Dart from the fabric store. Mrs. Dart wrote a letter for Sandy to include with her application, but because of the "hell" ("this little girl is one hell of a talent," Mrs. Dart wrote) Sandy couldn't send it. Mrs. Dart turned up at the funeral and was rushed to a chair by Aunt Betty, who thought her shakes were heatstroke.

Sandy's hands rise to cup her belly. "Of course I'm not going," she says.

"It's not too late for an abortion," Lou says.

"Quit saying that," Norma says, and Sandy, gazing down at her stomach so lovingly you'd swear she could see in, says in a far-away voice, "What a thing to say."

"What a thing to *do,*" Lou says.

It rains the next day, ending the heat wave. Their father shaves, puts on a clownish green-and-red checkered suit and a grey fedora, neither of which he's worn in ten years, and sets off for work.

After breakfast none of them goes into the wake room. Sandy returns to her bedroom and draws designs for baby clothes, one after the other, draws fast and yet still can't keep up with her inspirations. Norma does nine days' worth of dishes, then calls the hardware store to say she'll probably be at work tomorrow. Then, forgoing the squeegee mop, she gets down on her hands and knees and washes the kitchen floor.

Lou slouches in the kitchen doorway. She smokes their father's Export A's. She feels pensive and restless. Before breakfast, by mistake, she answered the phone "hello." Her thoughts are leaning languorously toward formulating some big plan for her future.

By lunch time the three of them are back in the wake room. They miss the room and each other in it, and they miss being where their mother's ashes are. They're feeling pretty good, though, until the channel eleven matinee comes on—*Seven Brides for Seven Brothers,* a delightful tune-filled yarn, according to the *TV Guide,* but it turns out to be one of the worst, most depressing movies they have ever seen.

"Go fuck calves," Lou yells at the screen when one of the brothers rejects one of the brides by bellowing, "Beautiful eyes, but what a size!" Lou feels as though it's Norma she's defending.

Part of Lou's irritation is that a moment before, they heard the front door opening. "What are you doing home?" she says when their father appears in the doorway.

He isn't drunk. His eyes blaze, but they're focused. For the first time since their mother died, he enters the room. He strides over to the TV and picks up the ashes. "It's time to scatter her," he says. He holds the box in both hands, up by his chest.

"Do we have to?" That's Sandy. Now that she's about to be a

mother, she doesn't recognize his exclusive right to the part of their mother that was her body.

"Where?" Lou asks their father.

"Niagara Falls."

Norma reaches the car first and climbs in the back seat. For the last year and a half, anytime she's had to go somewhere with their father, and he's driving, she's climbed in the back seat. Now it's habit. Sandy climbs in next to her.

"Thanks a lot," Lou says, getting in beside their father. In Lou's case, it's just her lifelong aversion. She has no idea about him making a pass at Norma. Norma would never hand Lou that much ammunition.

On the seat between Lou and their father is the box of ashes. Lou goes to pick it up, but their father growls, "Leave her." After a few minutes Lou switches on the radio and finds the FM rock station. She even lights a cigarette. He doesn't say a word.

By some magic every song on the radio is in time with the windshield wipers. Lou leans against the door and takes a hard look at their father. She still hasn't figured out why she never turned him over to the police.

He's handsome, she has to admit that, even featured, a strong jaw, but his mouth curves down like the mask of tragedy, and his eyes are the last word in unhappiness, in anger, in craziness. Lou sees all three aspects sequentially. She always sees them (though not always in that order) when he's sober, and maybe it's not being able to decide which aspect is the real one that's kept her from squealing.

She sighs and shifts to look out her window. Let's face it, she thinks, she hasn't called the police because she can't be bothered, because she hasn't got the energy, and probably not the disloyalty, either, to pretend she has a case.

Premeditated murderer. She liked the sound of it. The shock value. But the truth is, all he did was screw up. It reminds her of when the cat climbed into the fan belt. It was their father's fault . . . but it wasn't his fault.

When she leaves home, she won't come back, not to see him, that's for sure. Hanging around him, she acts like him, she always has, so that for most of her life she's been somebody she can't stand. But when she leaves home, she is going to do something great. What? She has to concentrate. Everywhere since their mother died there seem to be signs, such as the windshield wipers clicking to the beat of every song. Such as the fact that it's raining so hard now you can't see ten yards in front of you, and all the cars are in a blind chain, trusting some driver miles down the road.

After about half an hour their father reaches over to the glove compartment and takes out a bottle.

"Oh, great," Lou says.

He drinks steadily and savagely for another half hour or so, until every trace of anger and craziness drains from his face and he looks nothing but unhappy. At this point Lou knows that he'll do what she says. She says, "Pull over."

He and Norma trade places. "What if he barfs?" Sandy asks, and she squeezes into the front seat, too, and holds their mother on her lap, an inch of flesh away from the baby. In the back seat he lies down. Luckily the rain has let up enough for them to read road signs.

"You had a roof over your heads," he shouts. "You had three square meals a day! By God!"

Lou turns up the radio.

Like anyone, the girls have seen lots of photographs of the falls, and they've seen the movie *Niagara,* with Marilyn Monroe. They expect to be wonder-struck. But through rain and from a distance the real thing is just a black-and-white picture. A confirmation that they've arrived at the right place.

Lou turns around to their father. "Where do you want to go?" she asks. "To the American side or over there?"

He pulls himself up. Norma slows down the car. "Not here!" he shouts at her. "Not here!" He leans over the front seat and points the whiskey bottle at the Horseshoe Falls. "Drive right to the end!"

"Keep your shirt on," Lou says.

"Right to the end!"

Norma pulls into a parking lot on a rise of land overlooking the road. The wind buffets the car. Only a few people ("Honeymooners," Sandy says beatifically) are down by the low wall that runs along the lip of the gorge.

"Shit," Lou says. "We forgot umbrellas."

"Where is she?" their father cries. Over the seat Sandy hands him the box of ashes. And then he's out of the car and hurrying, weaving, across the parking lot.

"He's going to get hit," Norma says, opening her door.

Before he reaches the road, Norma and Lou catch up with him. Norma takes his arm while they cross. He tugs like a dog. Behind them, Sandy, shawled in the car blanket, calls, "Don't throw anything 'til I'm there!" She isn't going to run and jolt her baby.

He leads them across the lawn to the wall. It's only about three feet high with another foot of railing on top. He goes straight to a spot where there's an inlaid plaque with words carved on it. He doesn't look at the plaque, but the girls do because their first thought is that it's about their brother.

"José Maria Heredia," Lou reads aloud. "Cuban poet. Exiled patriot called the sublime singer of the wondrous greatness of Niagara Falls." She looks over the wall.

They are standing directly above the falls, a hundred or so yards from the drop. In her imagination Lou always saw glassy water here, but the water races and tumbles like water already gone over. You can't see the falls. You see the upshot—a huge mist full of white gulls in Pandemonium.

Right where they're standing, the water doesn't reach the stone wall. There's a little bank of grass and small bushes. From where they're standing, unless you threw a thing, it would hit land.

Lou turns to their father. "Let's get the show on the road," she says.

He's trying to open the box.

"Throw the whole thing, why don't you?" Norma suggests.

He continues struggling with the clasp.

Lou snatches the box away. "Here, I'll do it." From having opened it a couple of times at home, she knows how to undo the clasp. As soon as she flicks it up, he grabs the box back.

"Lean over the railing," Lou instructs him. The wind is coming hard off the water, and she's afraid that the ashes will blow back in their faces.

He leans, then throws the whole box anyway. Some ashes spill out and fly in a grey flock into the bushes. The box hits the water just inches from the bank. It capsizes, swirls, sinks, pops up. The girls hold their breath. Their father grips the railing. They are all pulling for the box.

When it goes over the falls, Sandy makes a sound of loss. A seagull echoes the sound.

"Okay," Lou says. "Let's go." She's soaked and shivering.

"Come on, Dad," Norma says gently.

He growls and waves her away. From his jacket pocket he extracts the whiskey bottle.

"Just leave him," Lou says. "We can wait in the car."

"He can't cross the road by himself," Norma says.

"We can watch from the car. When he starts heading back, you can run out and get him."

They turn on the engine for the heater and the radio. The only station that comes in clearly is an American one playing blasts from the past. "Mr. Sandman." Until their father comes back, Sandy is lying in the back seat. She's exhausted.

Lou, leaning against the passenger door, is the one who has a view of him. She pushes in the lighter and fishes in her sweater pocket for the cigarette she felt in there a few minutes ago. It's not a cigarette, though. It's a partly smoked joint. "Hey!" she rejoices, holding it up. She doesn't remember, but she must have pocketed it one of the times she was with Tom.

Norma and Sandy are shocked. No way, Sandy says when Lou suggests the three of them smoke it. Norma asks if it'll make them go wild. She envisions herself driving the car over the falls, and she also wonders if they have an explanation here for Lou's personality swings. Nah, Lou says. Marijuana just makes you feel good, high, like you've had a few drinks, only better. She lights the joint, takes a drag, extends it to Norma. Norma sighs. A capitulating sigh, Lou rightly judges. She puts the joint right at Norma's lips. Norma inhales.

"That's the spirit," Lou rasps without releasing breath. She takes another drag, then passes the joint over the seat to Sandy.

"I better not," Sandy says.

"The womb acts like a screen," Lou rasps, "keeping out harmful substances."

"How do you know?" Sandy watches Norma take another drag. She's starting to feel left out.

"I know everything. Come on. This is a big day."

With Lou holding the joint, Sandy sits up and takes a prim little puff. She coughs it out.

"Try again," Lou says. "Suck in air at the same time."

After a few minutes Lou lowers her window an inch. Leaning back against her door, she laughs. "What a suit," she explains, nodding over Norma's shoulder.

Norma turns around to look at him. "He's going to catch pneumonia," she says. Then she laughs, too. "It's a pretty awful suit, alright."

"A nice silk and wool blend, though," Sandy says professionally. Lou and Norma are silenced. Then all three of them burst out laughing. They can't stop. Sandy holds her belly to keep it steady. But it trembles. Inside it trembles. "My baby's laughing!" she cries. Lou passes her what's left of the joint.

When they quiet down, Lou asks Sandy how someone as smart as she is, when it comes to clothes, anyway, can marry someone as moronic as Dave.

"He's not moronic!" Sandy cries. And for the first time she is positive that she loves him. Her baby stirs, settling. "Are you sure about the womb having a screen?" she asks.

"Anyway, she's carrying his child," Norma points out. Her mood plunges. The only comforting thought is that a baby has tiny lungs. "He'd have drowned right away," she says softly.

"Who?" Lou says, snapping her fingers to "My Kind of Town."

"Our brother."

"Oh," Sandy says as if the wind's been knocked out of her. An invention occurs to her—lengths of shammy straps that you wrap around yourself and your baby to bind the two of you together.

"Must have been quite a throw," Lou says in a quiet voice.

"We don't know that!" Norma says heatedly. "It didn't necessarily happen exactly where we were!"

"The newspaper said it happened where there was shore. I remember that."

"Well, I remember it said there were no witnesses."

"Why would she throw him, anyway?" Sandy cuts in. "She'd never throw her own baby. You don't know, Lou. You've never had a baby. She wouldn't." Her voice breaks. "Why *would* she?"

"To put an end to the Field line," Lou says.

"Oh, right," Norma says bitterly. "I can just see Mom deciding that. If she really threw him, it was temporary insanity. I've read about this. It happens to some women after childbirth. Temporary insanity. It's just a few seconds of not wanting a baby."

"I'm not saying she didn't love him," Lou says, and a thought that she had at the funeral parlor returns to her, and she adds, "Probably she loved him too much."

"It was temporary insanity," Norma says.

"She wouldn't throw him," Sandy insists.

"Okay, okay," Lou says. Her sisters' first time smoking is turning into a downer.

Norma gets out of the car, slams the door and runs across the parking lot toward their father. The way she runs, Lou thinks fondly, is the way she is: restrained, determined, not-too-fast. Lou smiles at Sandy. "Has your little baby stopped laughing?" she asks.

Sandy curls up on her side and pulls the blanket around her. "I thought up an invention," she says.

"Oh, yeah?"

While Sandy describes some incomprehensible bondage contraption, Lou watches Norma and their father. He doesn't budge. He doesn't turn his head. Norma points at the car, then starts running back to the accompaniment of Nat King Cole singing, "If I Had to Choose Just One Day."

A gust of rain comes into the car with Norma. "He wants us to drive home and leave him," she says.

"Good idea," Lou says. But she smiles to show she's kidding.

Norma combs her fingers through her short hair, spraying water. "Go on and kiss her," Nat King Cole sings. "Go *on* and kiss her."

Kissing Stella returns to Norma so vividly, so physically that she has to close her eyes. She takes off her glasses and lies back on the head rest. She has settled with herself that what happened between her and Stella can't be compared to what happened between herself and their father (for one thing, Stella isn't related to her; for another, she was in love with Stella). All the same, she realizes that from Stella's point of view, the two events wouldn't seem all that different. Norma suspects that unconsciously she must have wanted Stella to grow up. "I know," Stella said when Norma cried, but *what* did Stella know? Norma measures her own life by the change she saw in her face the day their father made the pass. She thinks about seeing the change a lot more than she thinks about the reason for it.

Their mother dying has changed her again. She knew this when she accepted the marijuana cigarette. Why not? she thought, watching Lou inhale and imagining their mother floating up to heaven, unburdened enough and brave enough to float because of having nothing left to be afraid of.

Lou is humming in a distant, off-key way that Norma takes for mourning and that makes her sad. But she also feels as if she is floating, as if she and their mother are holding hands. "I wish," she says, "we could drive to Disneyland. Right now. Just drive south and west, south and west, 'til we got there."

"Let's hit the road," Lou says.

Her eyes still closed, Norma smiles.

Lou glances at the back seat and sees that Sandy is asleep. She switches off the radio.

The rain falls softly in grey, bad-television-reception lines. Everything that Lou is looking at is grey and dirty white. Except for their father's ridiculous green and red suit. The typical used-car-salesman's suit. She remembers him going off to work in that suit and that hat. His confident, military walk to the car. On the lookout for the neighbors' slip-ups. It's no compensation, Lou thinks, addressing him, referring to what she figures would be his defense of those grey years: "Nobody can that say Jim Field didn't own a colorful outfit!"

Norma is asleep now. Snoring. Dead stoned, Lou thinks and is reminded of when the sight of Norma at the end of the street made her want to cry and then made her want to make Norma cry. How could she have been so mean? To Norma, of all people? Look at her asleep there. Her kind, plain face. A saint's face, Lou thinks, good and kind and unprotected by beauty.

Their mother was good and kind *and* beautiful. Lou smiles at the thought that she used to get their mother mixed up with the Virgin Mary. Beauty was no protection against people dying on their mother, though. First her own mother died of a stroke, then a few years later her two brothers got killed in the war, and then a few years after that the baby died. If throwing the baby was just speeding up the inevitable, Lou wonders why their mother didn't throw herself, too. Of course, you could say that she did—she threw her life. And yet she didn't seem unhappy. Except. . . .

Lou remembers something. She has a revelation. Her heart begins to pound, and she rummages in her pockets for a cigarette, but she hasn't got any. She takes the roach out of the ashtray and eats that.

What she has remembered is the morning that she dropped acid, and their mother talking about an urge to be where the baby was when she let him fall. That's not exactly what she said, but it's what she must have meant. Because on the night she died the highest place she could get to was where she went.

Ever since swallowing Maternal Instinct at the funeral, Lou has believed that their mother loved the baby with a mother's blind love. Whether or not their mother threw the baby or dropped him, whether it was an act of craziness or sacrifice, whether or not all these years she has been sorry, it dawns on Lou that sometimes she must have been haunted by the moment at which she was standing at the railing, and there was the thunder of the falls, and her eyes were glued to the water that was on the verge of going over—nothing could stop the water now—and she had that weight in her arms. The moment at which the thing she loved enough to die for, she let die.

"I have to be up high," she said when she wanted to get up on the roof, when Lou and Norma tied her up with the skipping rope. Lou lets out an astonished laugh at the memory of tying her up. She wipes the windshield with her sleeve, but nothing happens, and she realizes that why she can't see out is because she's crying.

God, I'm stoned, she thinks, pressing her palms into her eyes.

The rain is suddenly falling hard again. Lou wonders about their father and leans forward to look out Norma's window. What is he doing? She sits straighter. What the hell is he doing?

Jesus Christ, he's climbing the wall!

She covers her mouth with a hand that smells of marijuana. God! He's got over! She pulls on her door handle. It's stuck. "Come on," she mutters, bumping the door with her shoulder.

Their father is walking down the bank.

"Come *on.*" She jiggles the door handle and hits Norma on the arm to wake her up. Norma moans in protest but doesn't open her eyes. All Lou can see now is their father's hat. He must be on the edge of the bank.

Lou starts to climb over Norma, and then it comes to her that her door is locked, not stuck, and she turns back around, pulls up the button, opens the door and jumps out. The rain is like a hose turned on her. "Dad!" she screams.

The only people anywhere near him are under a black umbrella, facing the other way. They don't hear her either. She runs across the parking lot and the road. A car throws up a wave of water, drenching her. The car behind it skids, honks. She screams "Dad!" again as the black umbrella moves away from him, as a seagull swoops down from the sky and circles above his head.

He just seems to be standing there. The seagull won't go. The seagull is their mother, Lou thinks, already reincarnated. Their father's hat tilts back, he's looking up at the sky, too, and suddenly Lou is overcome with such a strong sensation of his grief that she stops running.

For a few minutes she doesn't move, then she walks over to a tree, where the rain continues to pour over her. There goes their mother, flying off. Lou stays where she is. Even here across the lawn from him, she feels like an intruder. She watches his hat, which seems to be sitting on the water. A little houseboat. It doesn't tilt this time when the seagull flies back. The seagull who is their mother, Lou thinks. Right in front of their father, their mother dives into the water and shoots up with a fish, then soars into the mist, the fish drooping out of her bill. Lou shuts her eyes. She is getting that ecstatic feeling again, as if the rain is washing away her resistance to it, washing away whatever else she should be feeling, and all that's left is the sheer happiness she experienced up on the roof and in the washroom at the funeral parlor.

"Mommy," she says out loud, like a child, because the feeling of ecstasy is beginning to fade. But as it does, the idea grows in her that the reason their mother flew by was to give the feeling to her. A benediction, a legacy. Comfort from the other side.

A tremor passes through Lou's body. She starts crying. She runs back to the car, where her sisters are asleep. The rain feels hot, and her feet don't seem to touch the ground.